NEW WATER

TWELVE STORIES

ANTHONY ROBINSON

novels by ANTHONY ROBINSON

A Departure From the Rules

The Easy Way

Home Again, Home Again

The Whole Truth

The Member-Guest

The American Golfer

The Floodplain

CONTENTS

The 3-Mile Run, published in *Riverine,* An Anthology of Hudson Valley Writers, edited by Laurence Carr, 2007.

The Farlow Express, published in Prairie Schooner, Fall 1956, anthologized in The Best American Short Stories, 1957.

Zerk The Jerk, Produced by NBC-TV, Special Treat Series, 1985.

Cover photograph by Michael Hunold

Contact: tonytherob@gmail.com

ISBN-10: 149289849X

ISBN-13: 978-1492898498

For my sisters
Robin and Hala

NEW WATER

TWELVE STORIES

A BLUESTONE BOOK

THE THREE–MILE RUN

As I crossed our yard that drizzly afternoon, smoke was rising from the ground where my father, over the weekend, had burned out a tree stump. For the last couple of years he'd worked on making a lawn, and that meant clearing the ground. It was slow work and I didn't see much progress except for a patch of grass the size of our living-room floor. Our house sat among a lot of oaks and hemlocks and today, especially, looked sad and lonely. I had a feeling that something had happened. Had we lost another boy in West Harleyville?

I pushed open the front door, walked through the living room and into the kitchen. My mother was at the sink peeling potatoes. "Hello, Rupert," she said, not turning around.

I put my books on top of the big chest where we kept pots and pans. "Hi, Mom."

"How was school?"

"It was OK," I said.

I opened the refrigerator. When I turned around with a bottle of milk, she was facing me, drying her hands on her apron. She

1

had dark hair, pinned back like always. I grabbed a glass from the cabinet—

"Rupert," she said, "I have something to tell you. Sit down."

Only a month ago my mother had said the same thing, then had told me that Archie Beesmer's B-17 had gone down on a bombing run over Germany. We were good friends, went fishing together. Before going in, he'd given me his favorite lure, a silver Dare Devil with a ruby eye. A week after learning that his B-17 had gone down, I saw a gold star after Archie's name on the Roll of Honor in West Harleyville.

"This is very hard to say," my mother said, sitting down with me.

"Mom, just tell me, all right?"

She pressed her lips together. "Seth Nichols is dead."

I didn't say anything, just stared at her.

She reached across the table and covered my hand. "At first I wasn't going to say anything, but I spoke to your father and he said you had to know—we had to tell you."

"Mom, what are you saying? Seth's only—he's only fifteen. You can't join up at fifteen!"

"He committed suicide," she said.

"Committed suicide?"

"He hanged himself in their house in Chicago."

I gave my head a shake, close to crying. *"Why?"*

"They say he was very depressed, possibly because of the war. No one really knows." She was still holding my hand. "I'm sorry, Rupert."

We sat for a couple of minutes without talking. Then I told her I was going out.

"Maybe you should stay in," my mother said.

"I'm OK, Mom."

"Where are you going?"

"No place. Just around."

Outside, I moved aimlessly about the yard. With the smoke and the drizzle and the stumps, it had the look of a battlefield. I began walking up Rawson Road. On rainy or very cold days, back then, my mother would drive me to school in West Harley-ville, and we would always stop by for Seth who lived just up the road; but most of the time Seth and I walked.

It wasn't long before I came to the trail, the shortcut through the woods we'd taken so many times. I started along it, my thoughts spinning back to that spring day two years ago....

****

Mr. Myer had just rung the bell ending recess, and eight or ten of us left the field and began walking toward the school. Bill Vitone had the ball in his hand. Its cover had come off the day before, so he'd taken it home and wrapped it with black tape. He flipped the ball to Jimmy Osterhout who tossed it way up, then caught it behind his back. Showing off, like eighth graders were always doing.

The schoolhouse, a dingy yellow, sat on the corner of Hammond Street and Bonesteel Lane. The flag flew out front on a high pole, and parked under a maple was Mr. Myer's brown '42 Plymouth. We took the steps up, dropped our mitts in the hall and went in. Seth was already at his desk. Sometimes he came out at recess but he didn't like baseball or football, so he was never there when we chose up sides. When he'd first come to the West Harleyville school, last September, he'd said he was a runner; he ran "the distances." The kids had laughed. Jimmy Oster-

3

hout, who had a nonstop mouth, said the only "distance" Seth ever ran was the distance to the outhouse.

I sat down in the row for six graders and Jimmy and Bill went over to their desks, behind Seth's. Mr. Myer announced eighth grade science, to be followed by seventh grade math and then sixth grade geography.

I should've been studying New York State's lakes, mountains and canals but got wrapped up in the eighth-grade class instead. The topic was gravity. Mr. Myer was talking about Galileo's experiment from the top of the Leaning Tower of Pisa. What did the experiment prove? No one spoke. Then Seth raised his hand. It proved that gravitational pull was the same no matter what an object weighed, he said. He went on and talked about gravitational pull elsewhere. On some "celestial bodies" it was so strong a brick would weigh a ton. On other bodies you'd be able to lift a car. Personally, I didn't believe it, but Mr. Myer praised Seth for a full and excellent answer.

He turned his back to write on the blackboard and Jimmy Osterhout made a spitball and bounced it off Seth's head. Kids snickered, and Mr. Myer spun around. He had hollow cheeks and a sharp jaw, and he always wore the same dark-blue suit, shiny as coal. The spitball lay on the floor between Jimmy's desk and Seth's, and he told Jimmy to go to his office. Ten minutes later Mr. Myer walked down the aisle, went in and knocked Jimmy around for a couple of minutes. When Jimmy came back to his desk, his shirt was out and his hair was all mussed, but he had a smirk on his face and walked with a swagger. Mr. Myer wrapped up the lesson on science. It seemed like a good time for me to review what I'd studied last night at home, the Finger Lakes and the Erie Canal.

****

Five or six kids were standing on the corner when school got out at three o'clock. Jimmy was for playing a couple of innings but Bill said the bass in Dewitt Pond were beginning to hit. Fred Longo had taken down the flag, delivered it inside, and soon came out. He had big ears and stringy brown hair and was the only kid in the school I didn't like; he was for fishing. So Jimmy said, OK, fishing. Finally Seth came down the steps carrying his books. He was old-looking for thirteen, with reddish-brown hair and a large head and he wore knickers. He trudged over to where I was standing and we started walking away.

"Wait a minute," Jimmy Osterhout said.

"What is it?" I said, stopping.

"Not you, Rupert! *Him.*" Jimmy's small blue eyes leveled on Seth. "I'm calling your bluff."

"What on?" said Seth.

"That you're a distance runner."

"Call it, I don't care," Seth said.

"OK, let's do it then. We'll go around Bonesteel, then down Hammond and back to the school. Come on."

Bonesteel Lane curved back through the town like a huge horseshoe and hit Hammond Street four-hundred yards from the schoolhouse corner. It was a good mile and a half.

"All right," Seth said.

"Bill, you start us," Jimmy said.

"In two weeks," Seth said.

"What do you mean, *two weeks?*"

"We'll run in two weeks—only we'll go around twice."

Jimmy didn't say anything right away; he was thinking about it, maybe caught off guard. Then he said, "OK."

Seth and I started walking again, first on Hammond, then down a steep entranceway to Turner's Mill. I liked the smell of the sawdust and fresh-cut lumber. Past the sheds was a big open area where the trucks turned around—and beyond that point a big woods began. Last fall—the first week of school—I'd shown Seth the trail. If you took it, the walk to and from the Maverick Art Colony where we lived was fifteen minutes; by the main roads, over an hour.

The trail ran along a ridge of thick pines, then dipped, circling a swampy area where hundreds of dead trees stood, barkless, like skeletons. Maybe fifty crows were perched in the brittle gray branches of one tree, cawing away. Along the side of the trail, in a damp, shaded patch, pink flowers were growing, maybe two dozen in all. Earlier this spring, when we'd first seen the flowers, I'd told Seth they were called Lady's Slippers. What they were was wild orchids, I said. He wanted to pick one and bring it to his mother, but I told him they were protected by state law, so he left it alone. A limb moved up ahead in an oak. Gray, I thought. Then, sure enough, a big gray squirrel jumped to another tree. Seth didn't see it. He was walking heavily along, eyes lowered. Last fall, walking home one afternoon, he'd told me he didn't like what was happening in Europe. What was happening in Europe? I asked him. He said dark clouds were spreading across the Continent. In his opinion, we were headed for another world war. It was funny how someone could see dark clouds over Europe but not a squirrel in a tree.

A big fallen oak lay across the trail. We sat on it, as we often did. Seth's feet touched but mine had a couple of inches to go. Off to the right, in a grove of pines, stood a single white birch. It always made me think someone was standing there, watching us.

Seth sat bent over a little. By his expression, I thought he was probably seeing those dark clouds. "Rupert," he said, "I don't care whose side you're on. If you're for Jimmy, that's fine."

"I'm not for Jimmy." It scared me a little saying it but it was true.

We were quiet for a while. In the pines a squirrel was chattering. I knew it was a red by the sound, sharp and angry. A gray squirrel makes a softer, sadder sound, like someone crying.

"I'd like you to be my trainer," Seth said.

"Your trainer? I don't know anything about running the distances."

"What's there to know? You'll be on your bike, pacing me. Rawson Road's about a mile and a half from the colony to where it ends," Seth said. "That makes three miles, out and back."

I looked at the tops of my shoes, thinking about the West Harleyville kids, what they'd say if they found out. I could imagine, and I wasn't happy.

"What do you say, Rupert?"

"Well…sure."

"Great."

We shook on it, then got up and began walking again. The trail came out at the southern end of the art colony. We walked a short way and saw the first cabin. All the cabins had names. Up ahead was "Carpenter Shop." It had a steep roof and a sculptor, Carl Roja, lived in it. He carved big pieces of wood, weird shapes that didn't look like anything *I'd* ever seen. We came to the place where the artists, starting in early June right through to November, would meet for coffee or supper; it had a big screened-in porch and was called "Intelligentsia." A woman with caramel-colored skin ran it; her name was Christine. I liked stopping by when she was cooking up big crocks of goulash or chili. An old quarry separated "Intelligentsia" from the next house, called "Bluestone." It had an exterior of flat stones, fitted together like a jigsaw puzzle. Seth lived here with his mother and father. Two empty pails were sitting at the start of a short path leading to the house.

He almost stumbled over them but that was the idea. Seth set his books on a flat rock. I had nothing special to do so I told him I'd help. I grabbed one of the pails and we crossed Rawson Road, then followed a path past Lucy LeBlanc's house. She was an artist; in one of her paintings, now hanging in our house, nine or ten naked woman are sitting around a pool laughing and eating grapes and having a wonderful time. We came to a ridge. Here smaller cabins were scattered through the woods. These were taken by the actors and musicians and artists who came to the colony summers only. My parents and Carl Roja and Seth's parents lived here year round. We reached the pump. It was on the edge of a big yellow field, and at the end of the field stood a large building made of rough timbers and pine slabs. It was the Maverick Concert Hall. It blended in so nicely with the woods you might never know it was there. One of the pails wasn't completely empty, and Seth poured what was left down the throat of the pump, to prime it. The pump didn't have an ordinary handle but a big iron pipe, six feet long. Alone, I could hardly budge it.

We both grabbed the pipe and pressed down on it, again and again. After two nonstop minutes the water started flowing, and pretty soon the pails were full. The water was icy cold and Seth was sweating and he told me to keep the handle going while he put his head underneath; it was a struggle but I managed. Then he pumped and I got doused.

For a while we sat resting up in the sun letting our hair dry. A hawk was making a big slow circle in the blue sky over Ohayo Mountain. Finally we got up and I went to reach for one of the pails but Seth took both—"for balance"—and didn't stop once for a rest. We reached his yard. There wasn't a blade of grass anywhere—just pine needles. Seth was staggering. In a corner of the yard sat the Model T he was trying to make go again; an artist had left it behind five or six years ago as dead. Seth liked to say I was helping him, even though all I did was steelwool rusty parts and pass him tools when his head was buried in the engine.

I held the door to the screen porch and he set the pails under the drainboard in the kitchen, puffing away. Half the main room was his father's studio, the part under the skylight. I looked at the mural Mr. Nichols was working on. It was a train yard, all the engines and cabooses, the smoke and coal piles and turntables, the workers and engineers. I thought it was a great painting. Every time I looked at it, I saw something new. On a bench across from Mr. Nichols's paints and canvases lay newspapers and magazines, mostly from New York City. A Chicago paper came in each week, Seth told me, and every two weeks a London paper. And once a month a paper called *Le Monde* arrived from Paris. One time Seth read me an article in French. I didn't understand a thing but it was fun listening to him. He taught me three words, "bonjour," "merci" and "au revoir."

"I'll see you in ten minutes, Rupert," he said.

At home, I had a glass of milk and talked with my mother. My father was in New York. He was a poet but to make ends meet he wrote articles for magazines, and he was always seeing editors. We had our own well and the only inside bathroom in the colony.

I went back out, getting my bike from the shed. Seth was waiting for me by my parents' mailbox. Opposite the box was a small field surrounded by woods, and in the center of the field stood the Maverick Horse. A sculptor named Richard Flannery had carved it out of a dead walnut tree before I was born. It was rearing up, head high, ears back, a wild look in its eyes. My father said it was the symbol of the colony.

Seth told me to stay ahead of him by twenty feet; pacing a runner acted as an incentive, kept him going. "OK," he said, "start." He slogged along, head lowered, in an old pair of corduroys and black, ankle-height sneakers. Boom, boom, boom—he had heavy legs and he jarred the road each time a foot came down. After a while he said, "Move it—out—a little—"

I pedaled faster and Seth ran a little faster. Boom, boom, boom. But before long he was slowing down, face red, gasping for breath. At the intersection with Rt. 357, we stopped. He kind of leaned on me for a minute and I figured holding up the runner was part of a trainer's job. Then he put his hands behind his head, elbows out, and walked around a little. "OK," he said, "now back. We'll pretend—my mailbox is—the finish. When we get—to your mailbox—shout 'kick'."

"Kick?"

"It's an extra—gear—at the end of a race, a burst."

I turned my bike around and Seth started running again, soon panting fiercely. I heard a car; you could always hear one coming on Rawson Road, as far away as three miles. By the time of day and the tinny sound it made, it had to be Mr. Levitt in his Nash. It was; he gave us a honk. Seth was hammering the road and, at my mailbox, I yelled, "Kick!"

I didn't notice any change. So I yelled it again. "Kick!" Nothing.

The road made a small turn, and when we got to his mailbox—maybe two hundred yards from mine—he stopped running. He staggered and heaved, then clasped his hands behind his head and stumbled along.

"Do you want to sit down and rest?" I asked.

"No. You have to—keep moving."

I could hear the low thud-thud of Carl Roja's mallet through the woods.

"We have to—work on—my kick, Rupert," Seth said. "In running the distances—it's everything."

"Then that's what we'll do."

"Tomorrow, same time," Seth said.

A couple of days later Jimmy Osterhout asked me, as we were coming in from recess, if anything was going on with Seth. "What do you mean?" I said.

"Is he training?"

"Not that I know of."

Jimmy scowled; when he scowled he looked like a muskrat. "Walking together, he ever mention anything, like strategy?"

"Strategy?"

"How he's going to run the race."

"No."

"What *does* he say to you, walking back and forth?"

"Sometimes he'll ask me about this or that."

"Like what *this or that?*"

We went up the school steps. "Like a squirrel or a tree."

"What's the matter with you, Rupert?"

"Nothing. Why?"

11

"Forget it," Jimmy said. He gave me a hard, mean look. We tossed our mitts in the corner and went in. Seth was at his desk, reading a book. Mr. Myer announced Eighth Grade Science. I had a test coming up on New York State's waterways but I couldn't concentrate. I was trying to straighten out a couple of things in my mind, like whose side I was *really* on. Seth was my friend, but I'd known the kids in West Harleyville all my life. Later that day, coming home from school, I saw my father working in the yard. I wanted to talk with him because I knew he'd give me advice, but I didn't say anything. I just stood there watching him tend to a burning stump. Then I went in. It was something I had to figure out on my own.

Every day Seth ran and I paced him on my bike. After a week he didn't stagger so bad at the end and his face didn't get so red. But I still didn't see anything that resembled a kick, and I shouted it every time. Then, on Thursday, with only two days before the race, we trained extra hard, because Seth said on Friday we wouldn't do anything. A runner never trained the day before a race.

I pedaled and he thundered along. It was a hot day and the tar patches on the road were starting to bubble. Seth stayed to the side to avoid the tar. He was panting and sweat poured down his face; he was running pretty well, I thought. A whole lot better than the day we'd started. My mailbox was just ahead. I was about to shout "Kick!" But a car was coming down Rawson Road, drawing close, and I decided to let it go by first. It went by, and who had his head sticking through the open window, big ears and all, but Fred Longo.

"Your goose is cooked, Rupert!"

My wheels slipped on the loose gravel, and I went sprawling. Seth stopped running and came over. "You all right?" he said, heaving, his shirt soaked.

I sat on the side of the road, a couple of pebbles in my knee, clenching my teeth. I didn't say anything and Seth helped me up. "You'd better go in," he said.

I pushed my bike away, limping. My mother looked at the scrape and cleaned it with peroxide and put a gauze bandage on it. Friday morning I stayed in bed, telling her I felt sick. She took my temperature. Normal. Still she let me stay home. I thought about all the kids going up the school steps, talking, and how I didn't have the nerve to face them. About ten-thirty I got up and had a bowl of corn flakes and told my mother I was going out for a while. A man and woman were walking along Rawson Road with suitcases and artist equipment, looking for Bear Cub; so I offered to show them where it was. The woman was about twenty-five and had red hair; the man was a little older and had no hair at all. When we got to Bear Cub they invited me to come visit whenever I wanted. I walked on, stopping by "Intelligentsia" when I saw the door was open. Inside, sweeping and cleaning up, was Christine. We talked for a long while, and I helped her scrub the tables. Carl Roja was busy making his big wooden sculptures, and I went by Lucy LeBlanc's house and she was tending the flowers in her garden and waved and asked me why I was limping. I told her I'd taken a spill on my bike. Finally, I came to the pump on the ridge. I was thirsty but knew better than to try working the handle by myself. I walked out to the road again, passing Seth's mailbox; then, in front of my own mailbox, I stopped. On the other side of the road was the Maverick Horse.

I kept looking at it, wondering how anyone could make something so lifelike out of a dead tree, so wild and free. Then, all at once, I knew what I had to do.

The next morning, Saturday, I told my mother I was going to the school just to see some of the kids. She told me to take it easy, give my knee a chance to heal. It was hurting as I walked through the woods, then up the steep hill at Turner's Mill to Hammond Street; and then I never thought of my knee again. Maybe sixty people were gathered around Jimmy and Seth at the corner of Hammond and Bonesteel, and not just grade-school kids. High-school kids and parents, too. Bill Vitone was giving instructions to Jimmy and Seth. Painted on Hammond Street was a white line, which Bill said was both the start and the finish. They were to run twice around, as agreed. Jimmy was fidgety, anxious to get going. Both runners were on the line. Seth stood with his head lowered, in his corduroys and black high-tops, never seeing me. Then Bill said, "Get ready, get set." He hesitated, "Go!"

Jimmy shot ahead. Seth started out like he always did, steady, pounding the road. By the time they disappeared around the bend, Jimmy had a big lead. We waited for them to come around the turn on Bonesteel, on the far side of the big field, but it was only Jimmy we saw. He still had that springy step and the crowd started cheering. At last Seth came into view, and I gave out a big yell. Behind me, two women started talking. "His parents are Communists," one said, almost as if she wanted me to hear. "They're all Communists in the Maverick Art Colony," the other woman said. "There should be a law, it's not right they send their kids here." Jimmy turned at Hammond and ran on the straightaway. People were clapping, giving him encouragement. Seth

14

came along, head down. *Boom, boom, boom.* Still far behind, he started the second lap, the "gun lap," as he called it. Everyone was now staring across the field, waiting—then we saw them again, Jimmy still leading but Seth was closing. Where Bonesteel hit Hammond, both boys heaving, panting, their shirts drenched, faces twisted in pain, they were side by side. Everyone was screaming for Jimmy to hang on; and then someone yelled, "Kick, Seth! KICK!"

With six feet to go, Seth inched ahead and crossed the finish line a clear step in front.

Silence fell over the West Harleyville crowd like cold, heavy snow. Jimmy's legs gave out and he tumbled. Friends and class-mates clustered about him, and adults were saying "Give him air! Give him air!" The women behind me said I should be ashamed of myself, a look of hatred in their eyes. Seth stayed clear of the crowd, arms raised, hands behind his head, and after a while he went over and said something to Jimmy, then started up Hammond Street. What I did next took more courage than I knew I had. I ran to catch up with him.

After a while his breathing became steady and his hands fell to his sides. We went down the hill by the lumber yard and into the woods, passing the dead trees and the shaded spot where Lady's Slippers grew. We walked on; ahead, I saw the solitary birch among the pines, and at the fallen oak Seth said we should sit down and rest. He had something to tell me. The way he said it made me think it wasn't easy for him to say.

His father had received an offer to teach at a college in Chi-cago, he said, and they were leaving the colony. He thanked me for being his trainer. Seth dropped an arm on my shoulder. "I

15

heard you yell," he said. "It wasn't much of a kick, Rupert, but it was enough."

****

Now, two years later, the trail seemed different to me as I trudged along. Since Seth had left, I hadn't walked it once. Up ahead lay the fallen oak. When I got to it, I sat down, barely noticing that my feet reached the ground. For a long time I stared down the trail toward West Harleyville. Then I seemed to feel someone's eyes on my back. I spun around, and there, alone in the evergreens, stood the white birch. I went over to it and rested my head against it. From somewhere in the woods I heard the sad and lonely cry of a gray squirrel, but then I realized it wasn't a gray squirrel I was hearing.

GOOD FENCES

The closing on our new house was three weeks away and we would occasionally drive up from our Brooklyn apartment just to make sure we weren't dreaming. It sat on a quiet street in an upstate New York village, had a terrific view of craggy mountains from the rear deck, and was within walking distance of Lynwood State College where I'd recently landed a job as an associate professor of history.

Structurally the house, built before the Civil War, was sound. It needed a little work, standard stuff: a new roof, painting inside and out, a resetting of the brick pathway to the street. Otherwise it was perfect, if you overlooked—were able to overlook—our next-door neighbor's property.

His house was an uninteresting, all-brick ranch with an attached garage and a very large backyard, a full acre or more. If taken individually, the items in it were probably good serviceable stuff—a snowmobile and hitch, a flat-bottomed rowboat, a vintage John Deere backhoe, ladders of various lengths, half a dozen wheels with mounted tires, two barbecue grills (one gas, one charcoal), a score of window frames and storm doors, a high-wheel yard cart, a tilling machine, a gas-driven 3-wheel utility vehicle, a bass boat with a black Mercury outboard, a stack of criss-crossed railroad ties, and a pair of snow-plowing blades. Chained to a wire run that stretched between an oak tree and a white birch lay a graying short-haired German pointer, its house a flat-lying old whiskey barrel.

But I couldn't take these items individually. Removing the nice old dog from the picture, I saw them as a unit, and the unit spelled J-U-N-K. My wife didn't like the looks of our neighbor's property either, but we'd get used to it, she said. After a while we wouldn't even notice the stuff. On August 23 we moved in, spent the day unpacking boxes and pushing around furniture. Mid-afternoon of the second day we took our first real break.

I was seated in a director's chair on our deck, admiring the mountains (trying not to glance in the direction of our neighbor's yard) when Jessica came out with a pitcher of lemonade and two glasses. We talked about our house, which of the upstairs rooms would be the baby's (she was expecting in five months), and which of the downstairs rooms would become my study. As I was refilling our glasses, I noticed a man—tall, strongly built, with gray hair and a bristly gray beard, maybe 80 years old— crossing in front of our garage and coming toward our deck steps. In his large working-man's hands was a cardboard box filled with vegetables.

"Howdy," he said. "Junior Paulson's my name."

"Well, hello," I said, setting the pitcher down. "I'm Mitch Freeman. This is my wife, Jessica."

"Hello, Mr. Paulson," Jessica said.

"Thought you might want some tomatoes, some beans, corn's coming in real good. Got half a dozen ears here. Everything just picked." He set the box on the oak bench that we'd had in the foyer of our apartment.

Jessica was delighted. "Thank you very much."

"Welcome to Elting Road," Junior Paulson said.

"This is very thoughtful of you," I said.

He had on green pants and a green shirt, both sweat-stained, and a pair of work boots. "Not at all. We're neighbors," he said. "Well, I see you're making yourselfs comfortable, just thought I'd stop by—"

"Have a glass of lemonade with us," Jessica said.

"Well, it does look mighty refreshing."

She went inside and came out with a glass, which she filled. "Here you go, Mr. Paulson."

"Junior, just call me Junior."

"Sit down, Junior," I said.

We all sat down. "You got yourselves one wonderful house here," he said.

"Thank you, we really love it," Jessica said.

"Used to belong to my grandparents," Junior Paulson said, kind of looking around.

"Your grandparents lived here?" Jessica said.

"Sure did. It's the old parsonage. When the church let it go, my grandparents was the ones that bought it. Heck, I come out every summer when I was a boy. Ten years, never missed a summer. We lived in the Southern Tier but it was more fun here, big old rambling house." He smiled, had a swallow of the lemonade, looked around again. "This deck we're sitting on? Used to be a room. For city folk wanting to get away. When my grandpa died, my grandma begun taking in boarders—oh, could she cook!"

"That is all so amazing," Jessica said.

"Best years of your life, when you're a kid. Well," he said, finishing the lemonade, "I got quite a few chore waiting on me. Garden keeps you busy. Pretty soon now my grapes will be coming in. You need any help around the place, let me know."

"Thank you, Junior," I said.

"Well, enjoy the house—God bless you both," he said, and ambled down the deck stairs.

"What a wonderful man," Jessica said. "And look at these vegetables, will you?"

"They're beautiful."

"Mitch, we're so lucky, we have so much to be grateful for," my wife said. "What's an old backhoe or two?"

****

For the rest of the summer Junior brought over fresh vegetables once, sometimes twice a week. Winter came, and when it snowed he plowed our driveway as if it were his own. He also acquired, in that span, a beat-up drag-along camper, a dented aluminum canoe, and a "cap" for a pickup truck. My office windows looked directly across at Junior's land, and I was spending too much time looking at his stuff, cursing quietly. I was writing a book on a little-known aspect of the Reconstruction Era in Post-Civil War America, and it wasn't going well.

During our second winter we had a terrible cold snap in February, the thermometer plunging to 17 below one night; in the morning our pipes were frozen. I built a fire in the fireplace and Jessica sat in front of it with our baby daughter, Grace. I tried to get through to a plumber, any plumber, over and over again; no one picked up. It was pointless. Then, at two that afternoon, water started pouring through the basement ceiling! What to do? Junior! I called him and in minutes he was striding across our rear deck and made a beeline for the root cellar where he cranked shut the water-supply inlet valve. Then he commenced to make the necessary repair—first purging the system, then crimping and soldering the ruptured pipe. Five hours all told. I tried giving him a couple of twenty dollar bills but he flatly refused. It was what neighbors do, he said. They look out for one another. How about a drink? I asked. Yes, he'd have a drink.

That spring the trailer end of a tractor-trailer was pulled in and deposited behind Junior's house. It was a boxy, ugly thing, supported at one end by rusty struts. At least a log splitter served a purpose. I'd seen him, and heard him, use it: "Ker-*bammm!* Ker-*bammm!*" But a big old trailer with the word COASTAL across its side in red, 3-foot letters?

Several nights later as I lay awake—thinking how good Junior was to us and at the same time hating his yard—a solution came to me. In my mind's eye I saw the fence stretching the entire length of the property line, a thing of beauty—and functional to boot!

I was prepared for Jessica's objections when I told her, the next afternoon as she was feeding applesauce to our daughter, that I was going over to speak to Junior.

"About what?"

"About putting up a fence."

"A *fence?*"

"Yes. Professionally installed."

"Don't do it, Mitch."

"Jessica, that trailer is the last straw! It's an affront—"

"Things will never be the same, believe me," she said.

"True. They'll be better."

The baby started crying and Jessica, shaking her head, stood up and walked away with our daughter. I took a deep breath, gave myself a minute to reconsider, and left the house. Junior was just coming up from his garden—a large plot of rich, sunny land below his house—and, while waiting for him, I patted Maggie, his aging short-haired German pointer. My neighbor, in "county-green" shirt and trousers, invited me inside for a beer. "Inside" meant his garage. It was a den, without any plush furniture or TV or books. Just two canvas chairs tucked among shelves and shelves of tools, guns, fishing equipment, old steel traps, and mounted animals. On one shelf a red fox, on another a wild turkey, on another a bobcat. Above the glass-paneled door leading into Junior's kitchen, on an oval of black-walnut, was a 23-inch "trophy" smallmouth bass. Deer heads faced each other from opposite walls of the garage—one a handsome 14-point buck, the other an 18 pointer that had taken first place in the state's "Big Buck Award" forty years ago.

From a refrigerator in the corner of the garage Junior grabbed a couple of Budweisers. He snapped both cans, passed me one, said he had a new strain of tomato this year from Washington State. If I thought his tomatoes last year was good, just wait awhile.

I sipped my beer, then said I had something on my mind. He said neighbors had to be direct with one another, shoot. I had another swallow. "Junior--" I paused, started again. "Junior, I'm thinking of putting up a fence on the property line."

He looked at me straight on, no change of expression. "You want to put up a fence, go ahead."

"I wouldn't want you thinking Jessica and I don't appreciate what a wonderful neighbor you are, how generous and helpful you've always been—"

"It's a free country, Mitch. People do what they want."

"Well, I wanted to let you know what my plans are," I said.

"Glad you did."

An awkward silence followed, but then Junior was telling me he'd landed a 9-pound walleye on Shagg Pond last week, took him on the same red and white Dare Devil he'd had as a kid. Best lure ever made. His two daughters came over Tuesday with their families, cooked up the pike, they had themselves one fine dinner.

"It sounds really nice," I said.

I gave myself two days to change my mind. It didn't change. I picked "Holbrook Fencing" from our local Yellow Pages, and by week's end an 8-foot-high "privacy fence" ran all along the boundary line. To me, it served its purpose excellently, blocking out everything in Junior's yard except the top of the COASTAL trailer. Jessica—well, she liked the color of the fence, a deep forest green; other than that she said nothing.

How Junior was taking to it, I didn't know. Suddenly I couldn't see my neighbor moving about his yard, tending to his old dog, unloading his pickup. It was as if he no longer lived next door. Overnight, Junior Paulson, and his boats, trailers, hitches and utility vehicles, had disappeared from view.

Then, on a bright Sunday morning three weeks into our new protectionist lifestyle, as Jessica and I were reading the paper on our deck and Grace was playing in her pen, Junior surprised us by coming up the deck stairs holding a cardboard box. We exchanged a greeting. He said his garden was coming along real nice and he wanted us to have a sampling. He put the box on the hardwood bench. Nestled in it were half-a-dozen tomatoes, a couple of eggplants, two heads of lettuce and a large summer squash.

I was delighted—for more reasons than Junior knew. Jessica asked him if he'd like a cup of coffee; thank you, but he had chores. Carrots wanted thinning. He admired Grace, made a little chirping noise while looking at her, and went away.

"That's a relief," I said.

My wife didn't say anything.

"What's the matter, Jess?" I said. "He's showing us there are no hard feelings."

"I suppose," she said.

A week later Junior dropped off more tomatoes, even fuller and juicier than the first ones, with three cucumbers and a great bunch of carrots, tops intact. Like before, he didn't linger—his pole beans needed attention, they weren't looking too chipper. Jessica had taken Grace to the pediatrician, so she wasn't home. Shortly afterward, when she came in, she saw the produce on the kitchen counter and shook her head.

"Now what?" I asked.

"I wish he wouldn't do this," she said, holding our child.

"Darling, he enjoys giving us produce from his garden. Why do you keep questioning it?"

"He's killing us with kindness!"

"Come on, Jessica. Please."

Throughout the summer, on the average of once a week, fresh-picked vegetables appeared at our door. Jessica's reservations, doubts—whatever they were—faded. I kept thinking, especially when we had meals on our deck or walked around outside, that we had the best of both worlds: our privacy *and* Junior's friendship. The fence was working.

College opened for the fall semester. As I walked into the house, home after my first day of teaching, I spied a half-dozen ears of corn on the kitchen counter. Jessica, greeting me, said Junior had come by about an hour ago.

"Let's have a cookout," I said. "Corn on the cob and hamburgers."

I fired up the grill, made a couple of vodka and tonics, and we sat on the deck. It had been a beautiful day—clear blue sky, not too hot—and was now a gorgeous early evening. I told Jessica about my classes, described a new professor we'd hired with a specialty in medieval history; then we talked about a trip we were planning to take next month to visit her folks in North Carolina. We shucked the corn, admiring each golden ear. As I was putting on the hamburger patties, a deep, reverberating sound, like a big diesel turning over but not catching, filled the air.

"Rrrrggaahhhh! Rrrrggaahhhh! Rrrrggaahhhh!" Then, in thirty seconds, again. "Rrrrggaahhhh! Rrrrggaahhhh! Rrrrggaahhhh!"

"What's that?" Jessica said. It was coming from across the fence.

"Maybe Junior's bought himself a truck."

"That's a truck?"

"What does it sound like to you?"

"More like a bull."

We tried ignoring the sound but it was just too pervasive. Annoyed, we finished quickly. After carrying in our plates and utensils, I went down the deck stairs and crossed to the fence. "Rrrrggaahhhh! Rrrrggaahhhhh! Rrrrggaahhhh!" From this close the explosive force of the sound, always in sequences of three, was almost deafening. The close-tucked slats prevented me from seeing even the slightest movement. Then, from a short distance away, I heard Junior's voice. "Gettin' hungry, Tang?"

When he spoke again, he was directly across from me; without the fence, I could have touched his shoulder. "Good boy," he said. "Do you want to come in?"

There was a clinking of a chain, then silence. Back in the house, I told Jessica what I'd learned. It was a dog. Whether Junior owned it, or was merely helping someone by taking it for a couple of days, I couldn't say.

"Where's Maggie?"

"Jessica, we didn't speak. I don't know."

The next morning, and through the early afternoon, it was quiet on Elting Road. At 1:45 I left for the college to conduct a two o'clock seminar on the final days of the Civil War. When I got home the clock in the old church tower in the village was striking four. Responding to my inquiry, Jessica said she hadn't heard a peep from Junior's side of the fence.

"That's good news."

We had a cup of tea sitting together in the living room while our daughter played on the carpet. When we finished, I told Jessica I'd had a couple of good ideas while teaching and wanted to jot them down while they were still fresh in my mind. In my study, I picked up a pencil and began writing on a pad of paper—

"Rrrrggaahhhh! Rrrrggaahhhhh! Rrrrggaahhhh!"

"Oh, God," I mumbled.

"Rrrrggaahhhh! Rrrrggaahhhhh! Rrrrggaahhhh!"

I closed both windows but it was pointless. The bark was too loud. It buffeted the side of the old house like an angry March wind. I began pacing the floor, waiting for the animal to stop; waiting for Junior to come out and yell, "Shut the hell up!" But no. Frustrated and angry, I left my study and walked through the kitchen—

"Where are you going?" Jessica was preparing dinner.

"Over to visit Junior—"

"Mitch, be tactful."

—and out the back door. Down the deck steps. There was no longer a direct path between houses. To go from one to the other required circumventing the fence; to accomplish this, I walked out to Elting Road. Once around the fence I could see Junior's house. The overhead door to his garage was up, and standing in the doorway, almost as if he were expecting me, was my neighbor.

"Hello, Mitch," he said.

I approached him. "Junior, how are you?"

"Better now, I was feeling pretty blue. Maggie passed away."

"I'm sorry to hear that."

"But I got me a new dog," he said, his eyes lighting up. "Come on, I want you to meet him."

I could hardly wait. He led me through his garage, then through the conventional door that opened to his backyard. There, chained to Maggie's old run, was a brown and black dog of no discernible breed. I had expected an animal the size of a mastiff; this dog was only fifteen inches high. Barrel chest, thick neck, small leathery ears, narrow eyes. Teeth. Oh, he had teeth. Like a shark's. He was looking at me, head lowered, growling.

"Ain't he a honey?" Junior said.

27

I let the question slide by. "What kind of—dog is it?"

"Pit bull, mainly. A little Airedale. I got him off a retired dairy farmer up into Cooper County, him and his missus is moving to Arizona. He says to me, 'Give Tang a good home.'"

"Is Tang...friendly?"

"To me he is," Junior said. "I wouldn't recommend any stranger pettin' him."

"Why not?"

"He'd most take their hand off."

Junior picked up an old 2-quart saucepan lying on the ground, filled it with water at an outside hose connection, and walked over with it, emptying the water into a yellow bowl. Tang took a few laps, and Junior, reaching down, stroked his stubby ears. For some reason my eyes were drawn toward my house. All I could see of it was the nearer of its two brick chimneys.

"How about a beer, Mitch?"

"Swell."

We sat on the webbed chairs in his garage. I wanted to mention that I was finding Tang's thunderous bark disturbing, but I checked myself, hopeful the dog would stop on his own once he became better acquainted with his new environment. I drank my beer quickly, thanked Junior, and left. As I was walking out to the road, in order to circle the fence, he yelled after me that his Concord grapes were coming in; next week they'd be lush and juicy.

"Wonderful."

"I'll bring some over," he said.

****

He did, a whole grocery bag full. Tang kept barking. Usually he started about 5:00 in the afternoon and went until 7:00 or

7:30. The tension and stress began showing on Jessica's face, and I noticed the first gray (perhaps coincidentally) in my hair. In November our neighbor appeared at the our back door with a couple of venison steaks, nicely wrapped in butcher's paper.

"Thank you, Junior." I set the steaks on the kitchen counter. "Where were you hunting?"

"Up into Ulmer County, near Appleton," he said. "Jumped this 10-pointer, tracked him two hours in the snow. Figured I'd lost him, then there he come bounding down the Sawyerkill River creek bed. I nailed him with one shot from my ought-six."

Winter set in, the days grew shorter—dark by five. No problem for Tang; he started in at three. In January we had a heavy snow and Junior plowed our driveway. I almost wanted to go out and say to him, "Please, it's OK. You don't have to. Just *keep Tang quiet.*" That evening the dog's barking reached new volume, and Jessica said I had to do something. She was becoming a nervous wreck, she said, to the point of snapping at Grace.

At noon, the next day, I walked out to the road, then past Junior's WWII Jeep and F-150 parked in his driveway. When Tang saw me he started barking furiously, straining on his run. If his collar should break, the wire snap—I didn't want to think about it. I knocked at the back door to Junior's garage. "Hello, Mitch," he said, wiping his hands on a rag as I walked in. The engine to his tiller, dismantled, lay on his workbench. "Beer?"

"Sure."

"How was the venison?"

"We loved it."

"It was a fine buck," Junior said, going to his refrigerator. "Mostly these days you see spike horns." He pulled out a couple of Buds. "I'll never shoot me no spike horn. It's disgusting what hunters—they call theirselves hunters—will shoot today. Like a doe. I'd toss my guns right the hell in the river before shooting a doe. Cheers."

"Cheers." We were sitting in the web chairs. "Junior," I said, "there's something on my mind."

"We're neighbors, let's have it."

I took a breath and began. I was sure Tang was everything he wanted in a dog, I said. Loyal, intelligent, watchful. But he barked every afternoon, no little bark either. It was interfering with my work and generally causing stress in the household.

He seemed to have a ready answer. "Tang only barks when someone walks by on the road or pays me a visit."

"Junior, he barks every day for two hours, sometimes longer."

"You're hearing things, Mitch."

"That's true. Your dog. Maybe if you shout at him when he starts in—"

"I ain't shouting at Tang!" His eyes flared.

"Well, talk to him then," I said. "You could feed him earlier in the day, bring him inside earlier. Junior, really, it's unbearable."

"A dog that don't bark ain't much of a dog."

"Maggie didn't bark," I said.

"She was a field dog. Now I got me a guard dog. Anybody come snooping around here, Tang will tear their throat out!"

I almost gagged on a swallow of beer. "Junior, if that's what you want in a dog, fine. The fact is, he's disrupting our lives."

"I ain't getting rid of him, Mitch!"

"We don't want you to. All I'm asking—"

"He barks when people come to the house. Din't he just bark? How about now? Hear anything?"

Nothing more was said, and with the can of Bud half full, I left. Later that day Tang started in at 3:25 and went at it until 5:40. The next day was the same, and the next. Day after day. Jessica and I began arguing (about anything, about nothing), and Grace, instead of sleeping straight through, began crying at two and three in the morning—no little whimper either. We weren't a contented family in our house on Elting Road. Jessica expressed the view that maybe we should move.

"Move?"

"Mitch, I'm not happy here. Are you? When was the last time—?" But she didn't go on.

I wiped the sweat from the back of my neck.

"Either that, or we take down the fence," she said.

"Then we'd not only *hear* Tang, we'd see him!"

At that precise moment the good animal's quotidian attack on the peace and quiet on Elting Road commenced. "Junior's making us pay, you understand that," Jessica said.

"I disagree. You're reading too much into it."

"It's the fence, Mitchell. Read into it what you want!"

She walked out, and the next day I called the Mayor of Lynwood, thinking to ask if I was the only person in our beautiful village ever to have such a problem. As it turned out, the mayor was out of town until Monday; but his secretary, perhaps picking up the distress in my voice, asked if she could help me. I hesitated a moment, thinking it would be easier to simply call back. But then I was talking. Telling her my story. "I thought Mayor Terwilliger might be able to give me a little advice," I said. "Do I have any recourse?"

"There's a village ordinance on that very topic," the woman said.

"There is?"

"Oh, yes. Would you like me to read it to you?"

"If it's not too much trouble--"

"Hold on, the book's right here."

I could hear her turning pages. "All right," she said. "'Chapter 68, Paragraph B. *Prohibited Noises*. The keeping of any animal or bird which, by causing frequent or long-continued noise, shall disturb the comfort and repose of any person in the vicinity, is prohibited, providing the noise at the property line is over seventy-five decibels,'" She paused. Then, to me, "Is the barking over seventy-five decibels?"

I was jotting down notes. "It would wake the dead."

"Then you have a lawsuit."

"How do I proceed?"

"Just call the police. They'll issue your neighbor a summons, the judge levies a fine, and if the offense occurs again the fine is doubled. Then tripled. The fourth time it's a misdemeanor, and your neighbor could spend a year in jail."

"I really wouldn't want him going to jail—"

"It's unlikely, but that's the law."

My lips were suddenly parched, my throat dry. I thanked her and hung up. Just then, through the walls of the house, came the bark from hell. Jessica, in the living room with Grace, groaned. I glanced at my scribbles: "Vil. ord. Chap. 68, Par. B. Prohib. noises." Taking a deep breath, I dialed the police.

****

"Freeman v. Paulson" was the fifth case that evening before Judge Redford Hammond, a man in his 70s with rough skin,

coarse gray hair and a no-nonsense, call-'em-as-he-saw-'em reputation. Junior had on a clean, well-ironed set of county greens. I
spoke first, telling the judge that my neighbor's dog barked
every afternoon and into the early evening, destroying the peace
and quiet on Elting Road. A Lynwood police officer had responded to my call—but only after repeated efforts on my part to
have Mr. Paulson take action on his own, had failed. The officer
heard the barking and issued Mr. Paulson a summons.

Judge Hammond looked at Junior, indicating it was his turn.
My neighbor said his dog only barked when somebody walked
by his house; that was all he said. Then somebody, I told the
judge, would have to be walking by his house every afternoon,
continuously, for two hours.

Judge Hammond scraped his jaw. He was wearing a brown
shirt and a knit, maroon tie. It wasn't his practice, he said, to settle neighbors' disputes. He was referring "Freeman v. Paulson"
to nonbinding mediation.

"Your Honor," I said, "Mr. Paulson is in violation of Chapter
68, Paragraph B, of town law. In all honesty, I'm perplexed.
What is there to mediate?"

"Perhaps quite a bit, Mr. Freeman." Judge Hammond glanced
at the bailiff. "Next case!"

I fumed all the way home. Tang, sensing vindication, was
out-Tanging himself when I pulled into the driveway, got out
and shut (slammed) my car door. Seventy-five decibels? How
about ninety? How about a block-busting one hundred and fifty!

"Well?" Jessica said, when I walked in.

"The judge referred the case to mediation."

"Mediation?"

"Nonbinding at that."

Her head sank; in all the years I'd known her, I'd never seen my wife so stressed, preoccupied. I tried comforting her, unsuccessfully; she went upstairs to our room, closed the door. At my bar, I poured myself a drink; and soon went back to make myself another.

****

The Mediation Center was out on Vineyard Avenue, three miles from the village green. When I got there at 2:55—ten days after our appearance before Judge Hammond—Junior's F-150 was already parked in the driveway. The building was a big old farmhouse under towering locust trees. A tight flock of brightly colored bantam chickens was pinwheeling near the entrance. A woman about thirty-five, with smooth skin and dark, wavy hair, met me in the vestibule. Kids' coats were on hooks; boots lay on the stone floor.

"Mr. Freeman?" she said.

"Yes."

"I'm Carol O'Roehrs, the mediator."

Carrying a manila folder, she led me into a large room with a high ceiling and a polished wood floor; in the middle of it stood a conference table, also polished. I took a chair opposite Junior, and Carol O'Roehrs, in a long dress of faded denim, sat at the head of the table. She read the official complaint and the court's ruling. Then she looked at me and said, "Mr. Freeman, tell us what the problem is, as you see it. What would you like to have settled here?"

I began. When I finished, Carol O'Roehrs made a few notes and turned to Junior, asking him what his response was. He repeated his old line: Tang only barks if someone is walking by.

"And there's no proof his bark is seventy-five decibels!" he continued. "When the cop come out, did he have a device on him for measuring sound? I shouldn't of got the summons, because there was no proof it's over seventy-five decibels! No one took measurements. Plus the trees. Mr. Freeman says my dog is barking. Well his hemlocks is dropping pitch all over my vehicles—and I'm within my rights. Chapter 37, Paragraph C, Lynwood Village Law! I want them boughs cut back."

"Mr. Paulson, we're here to discuss your dog," the mediator said. "Mr. Freeman's trees are a different issue."

"Well, you can't find a better dog nowhere," Junior said. "He needed a home, a retired dairy farmer up into Cooper County, him and his missus was leaving the area—all they wanted for Tang was a good home. I looked at the dog and patted him, right off he licked my face, farmer never seen nothing like it, how we took to each other. Without Tang I don't know what I'd do, we sit together evenings and he sleeps in my room at night. Tang is the best damn dog that ever lived and I ain't getting rid of him because some *college professor*—" his eyes flicked across the table, taking me in, "—says he's barking too loud!"

"I never said get rid of your dog, Junior. I'm only asking you to keep him quiet."

"Asking me?" He spit out the words, his face deepening in color.

"Yes, asking you."

"By calling the police! Is that asking?"

"Calling the police was a last resort."

"Your dog," the mediator said, looking at Junior, "barks mostly in the late afternoon and early evening, according to the complaint."

"Tang barks when somebody comes to the house!"

"How often do people come to your house?"

Junior shifted positions in his chair. "Every day someone comes over. Maybe a couple of people will stop by—it depends."

"Then your dog would only bark occasionally," the mediator said. "Mr. Freeman says he barks nonstop for two hours, sometimes longer."

"Mr. Freeman likes to stir up trouble."

"How? Can you explain that?" the mediator asked.

"Ask him to explain it."

"Junior, I've never done anything to intentionally stir up trouble," I said.

"What about the fence?" he blurted out, veins in his neck swelling.

"I talked to you before doing anything," I said.

"With your mind made up!"

"What fence are you referring to, Mr. Paulson?" Carol O'Roehrs asked.

"The fence he put up between the houses."

"Which houses?"

"My house and his house, what he *calls* his house."

"What does that mean?" the mediator asked.

Junior paused for a moment, then continued—not to the mediator, not to me. He spoke, as if the words were coming from a well, a deep, hidden place. "Every summer when I was growing up my mother would put me on a bus to visit my grandparents here in Lynwood. We lived in Lewis Falls seventy miles to the west, a factory town, and Lynwood was a nicer place, plus my grandparents lived in a wonderful old house on Elting Road. My granddad always said there was a tunnel in the root cellar—runaway slaves used it coming up from the South—it was part of an Underground Railroad, and me and my friends in Lynwood found it—what was left of it, and some relics. Jimmy Longendyke found an old boot and Red Osterhout a brass buckle. My granddad kept pigeons in the loft over the garage, homing pigeons and tumblers, I tended them for the summer—I knew them by sight, every single one. Then he died and my grandma told me, on my last visit just before I volunteered for the army in '42, 'Junior, I'm leaving this house to you,' she said. 'Your mother don't care for nothing but herself—I'm leaving it to you. To live in and raise a family in when the war's over. That was the way it stood until she took ill and needed money. What she done, she split up the property into two parcels. Five and a half acres went with the house when she sold it. That gave me three and a half acres to build on next door, which I done. I wasn't happy how it all turned but I always enjoyed looking at the house, sitting there amongst them big maples so proud, thinking back to those early days. My missus would sometimes say things like how it wasn't fair but I never bore no grudge against the people living in it until some newcomer come over and told me he din't like what he saw in my yard and was putting up a fence! I didn't get the house but I always liked looking at it, like I said, and suddenly all I could see was a chimney! My dog barks. You're god-damn right he barks, he don't like the fence either!"

Silence settled upon the room. Then Carol O'Roehrs said, "Mr. Freeman, would you be willing to trim your hemlock boughs if your neighbor agreed to monitor his dog?"

"Yes."

"Mr. Paulson?"

"I'll see what I can do," he said.

"Can you be more specific?"

"I'll stop Tang if he starts barking."

"When, after how many minutes?" I asked.

"Mr. Paulson?"

"Let him say."

"What would seem fair to you, Mr. Freeman?" the mediator queried.

"Five minutes."

"Mr. Paulson, is that all right with you?"

"Whatever he says."

The mediator wrote a couple of lines on a sheet of paper. "Mr. Freeman," she said, "I'm asking you to have your hemlocks trimmed at the earliest possible time. Mr. Paulson, starting today I expect you to stop your dog from barking after five minutes. "Now," she said, looking first at Junior, then at me, "can you two men stand up and shake hands?"

We both got to our feet. I extended my hand but Junior left the table, never giving me a glance. He looked weary, not the weary that comes from tilling a garden or splitting logs or repairing a pipe ruptured in five places on a sub-zero Sunday afternoon; but soul weary. Carol O'Roehrs and I talked for a few minutes. My only official recourse, she told me, if Mr. Paulson didn't live up to the agreement, was to start over again by calling the police. "But I think he'll comply."

"I hope he will."

****

Later that same afternoon, Tang started in. I looked at my watch. 5:25. I sat down on the deck steps waiting to hear Junior come out of his house and silence his dog. By 5:40 there was no action on Junior's part, and I began to despair. At six o'clock Tang was operating under a full head of steam. I was ready to kill—dog or man, it didn't matter. Of all the stubborn, ornery, recalcitrant individuals in the world, Junior Paulson took the prize. Jessica came out of the house with a bawling baby and began yelling at me. I yelled back, telling her to take Grace and go for a drive! She turned away, angrily. It occurred to me she might take Grace for a drive and not bother coming back at all. I stomped around the rear deck for a couple of minutes, at a loss. Then it came to me. There was only on way to end this: I had to go over and have it out with Junior Paulson once and for all.

I circled the fence; his garage door was down and I walked around to the back. Tang saw me, immediately lunging—the wire twanged, vibrated; the leaves on the white birch quivered. I ducked through the conventional door and knocked on the door beneath the trophy bass. No answer. I knocked again, louder, and peered inside. Then stared inside. Junior was lying face down on the floor in his kitchen, in the same clothes he'd worn at mediation, one arm stretched out, the other beneath his chest.

The door was open and I went in, kneeled beside him; he wasn't breathing. I stood, went to the wall telephone near the door and called the police.

I gave my name. "Hurry! My neighbor is lying face down on his floor! 165 Elting Road!"

****

A Lynwood policeman—three squad cars were parked out front—asked me what I knew. Mr. Paulson and I had been at a mediation hearing at four o'clock over the barking of his dog. When the meeting ended, he walked out; next time I saw him he was lying here on his kitchen floor. The officer, a sergeant with swarthy skin and a big mustache, took notes. All the while Tang barked and barked. In time the county medical examiner arrived, and soon afterward attendants wheeled Junior's body in a brown vinyl sack to a black station wagon on Elting Road. I overheard one policeman say "dog warden" to another. Then the cruisers drove off. Alone on Junior's property, I sat on a couple of mounted truck tires while Tang strained at his lead, nails digging into the dusty ground.

"Rrrrggaahhhhh! Rrrrggaahhhhh! Rrrrggaahhhhh!"

"Tang, come on. What's the matter, boy?"

"Rrrrggaahhhhh! Rrrrggaahhhhh! Rrrrggaahhhhh!"

"It's OK, Tang."

After ten minutes his barking diminished, then stopped altogether. His tongue, hanging out, seemed swollen. He dropped into the dirt; though quiet, he eyed me distrustfully.

His water bowl was empty. I saw the old saucepan, went over and filled it, then looked at Tang. I ventured toward the run, talking quietly. "Good dog. Good boy, Tang." He got up but wasn't lunging or barking, and I emptied the saucepan into the yellow bowl. Tang drank for a full minute. "Good boy," I said again, thinking to extend my hand and pat his head; but that same moment a pickup truck pulled into the driveway. A man about forty, in heavy boots, canvas pants and a flannel shirt, stepped out and walked toward the backyard.

Tang started in. "Rrrrggaahhhhh! Rrrrggaahhhhh! Rrrrggaahhhhh!"

The man introduced himself as Monroe Sliss, dog warden. Tang was suddenly his old self again and, wary, I left the immediate area of his run. I told the warden I was Mr. Paulson's neighbor.

Sliss gave me a nod. He had bony hips and wide, skeletal shoulders; fastened to his broad leather belt was a sheathed hunting knife with a stag handle. He sized the dog up, then asked me if I could give him a hand. "My wife, we usually work together—she just come down with the poison ivy on her wrists."

I didn't say yes or no, and Sliss returned to his truck. In the payload area was a wire cage. He grabbed a muzzle and shoved it in his rear pocket, then dragged out a long metal pole with a loop of stout cord dangling from the tip. He yanked back on the forward section of the handle, tightening the noose, then loosened it. In a semi-crouch, Sliss moved in.

"Rrrrggaahhhhh! Rrrrggaahhhhh! Rrrrggaahhhhh!"

The warden stopped three feet shy of the clawing animal, deftly dropped the loop over his head and tugged back, grunting. Tang's eyes bulged; his tongue jutted between his teeth.

"Here," he shouted, handing me the pole, "keep her taut!"

He thrust it at me and I kept the pressure steady. Sliss dropped to his knees and slipped the muzzle over Tang's head. He unsnapped the chain to his collar and gave me a sign to release the handle. He lifted the noose around Tank's neck and, picking up the dog, shoved him bodily into the cage. "Thanks for helping," he said; he took the pole, secured the tailgate, and drove away.

I watched his truck disappear down Elting Road. Standing in Junior's backyard, I looked around at his bass boat with the black Mercury outboard, the log splitter, the old doors and ladders and windows, the snow-plowing blades and the COASTAL trailer. Tang's chain, hanging loose from the wire, still swayed. My eyes continued wandering, then settled on the fence.

I walked up to it, then, on impulse, began pushing. I used my shoulder, my arms and feet, shoving, kicking at the fence, weakening it by degrees, and at last one small section of it fell. Passing through the opening, I stumbled toward my wife and daughter standing by the house where Junior Paulson had spent the summers of his early life and runaway slaves had once followed a tunnel to freedom.

JUNK ART

At the New Falls landfill, Charlie Connable began emptying his station wagon of the stuff he'd taken from the loft over his garage. A few of the items would make for a good yard sale but he didn't want to bother; he just wanted to get rid of the stuff as so much junk accumulated during his marriage. Now, two years since he and Priscilla had divorced, he was cleaning out the loft at last. His children would soon be arriving in New Falls to spend the summer with him as part of the agreement, and he didn't want a repeat of last summer's circus. They were good kids but their hometown friends would come over and Charlie had gotten tired of the loud music and general noise and his own short temper, and he didn't want to go through it again. He was in the process of making a den for himself where he could read, smoke his pipe and, if the opportunity were ever to present itself, entertain.

He tossed two broken chairs on, or near, the "burn pile," followed by a wobbly card table, his ex's old vanity, a couple of carpets she had thought they might one day use, a handmade bookshelf from an earlier house they had owned. Also a couple of tired suitcases, a wooden stepladder with a busted rung; and, finally, a cracked easel and seven unframed oil paintings of no worth, dating to a time five years ago when he and Priscilla had first bought the house in New Falls. The previous owner, an artist, had left behind the paintings and easel in her studio—what Charlie now called the loft—telling him personally that she would come back for them. She never had.

Charlie brushed off his hands, got into his wagon and drove the three miles back to his house, where he climbed the steps into the loft and looked around. With the first job—clearing away the clutter—done, he contemplated the various steps to complete the project. Sitting in an old oak chair, the only thing he hadn't taken, he had a vision of the finished den. A select little bar against the wall, a pair of fine built-in bookshelves, a sound system—

But he cut short the fantasy; he had work to do. The next step, he judged, would be the windows. Many of the individual panes were loose. Charlie went back down the stairs and gathered together the necessary tools, positioned a ladder against the outside of the garage, and started in—first scraping away the desiccated glazing compound, then tapping in push-points and applying fresh compound. But there wasn't much in the can and he soon ran out. Needing other items as well, he drove to a Majestic's, a family-run hardware store set up in a refurbished old barn. He bought glazing compound, a folding ruler, a roll of masking tape and a razor-sharp knife with a retractable blade. As he was carrying his basket to the counter, he detoured down the paint aisle. He liked colonial colors, Majestic's carried a full assortment of paints, and perhaps he'd get an idea—

Standing at a case of fine-tipped brushes was someone he knew but couldn't place, a really good-looking woman at that. Not wanting to stare, he broke away to take in paint colors, only to realize who she was. None other than the previous owner of his house, Janet Summersell, whose paintings he had just ignominiously tossed at the town dump. Mortified, he started backing quietly away, but she spotted him and said, "Charlie?"

He feigned surprise. "Janet!"

She came toward him in avocado jeans and a pink shirt rolled at the cuffs. "How are you?" she asked. "It's been a long time—"

"Since the closing in New Falls Savings," he said, remembering how he'd felt attracted to Janet when he and Priscilla had first met her at her house; a month later at the bank his feelings for her were still there, in no way diminished.

"My God, how time flies!" she said. "I've often wondered how you were doing in the house."

"It's a great house, I love it," Charlie said. "My wife loved it also but, well, she had other lives to lead. We're divorced."

"I'm sorry to hear that."

"How are you, Janet?"

She was holding a couple of small brushes and Charlie caught a glimpse of her ring finger, the smooth nakedness of it. "I'm doing the best painting of my life," she said. "Critics are being very kind."

"Wonderful," Charlie said. Moving to a safer topic, he asked her where she was living.

"In Taos."

"I don't know much about it."

ANTHONY ROBINSON

"It's an exciting, beautiful place, a great art center, and the climate in New Mexico is fabulous." She smiled, then said, "I almost called you the other day."

"I—I'm sorry you didn't," Charlie said.

"I'm having a show in Santa Fe later this year," Janet said. "It's not a retrospective but the curator wants me to include some of my earlier work. By some remote chance do you have the paintings I left in my studio—I should say 'never came back for.' There might be a few I could use."

Charlie swallowed hard. What craziness had possessed him to chuck her work? But it might not be too late. Unlike the other stuff, he hadn't thrown the canvases onto the actual fire. If he raced back—

"I do, yes."

"How wonderful!" A light came into Janet's smoky brown eyes. "Charlie, you're a dear." She came in closer and hugged him, gave his cheek a soft kiss. "May I come by?"

"By all means."

"How's Monday?"

Monday he'd be in court all morning and he had meetings after lunch. "Sure. Four o'clock?"

"I'll be there," Janet said.

Charlie paid for his purchases and made a beeline for the landfill; it closed today at noon. The same man who'd given him instructions earlier sauntered out of his trailer. A toothpick stuck out between caked lips. "What can I do for you, Mac?"

"The stuff I unloaded earlier?" Charlie said. "I made a mistake leaving the paintings. I'd like to take them back."

"You're a little late," the man said.

46

Charlie glanced at his watch. "It's isn't twelve yet. What are you talking about?"

"After you left, a kid drove in with a shitload of burnables in his pickup. When he came back out, he had the paintings."

"What?"

"I was standing right there and seen 'em, stacked up real nice."

Charlie let out a choice oath. "Why didn't you stop him? It's a regulation, signs all over the place. 'NO PICKERS!'"

The man switched the toothpick from one side of his mouth to the other with a deft flick of his tongue. "What can I tell you, Mac? Who the fuck throws away paintings?"

Charlie rubbed sweat from his forehead. "You wouldn't know who it was who took them, would you?"

"It was a kid. I seen him before, don't know his name."

"What color pickup, what make?"

"Toyota. Kind of a washed-out blue, maybe a gray."

"Thanks."

At home, Charlie didn't finish the windows in the loft. He sat on his deck, thinking, wanting to come up with a rational explanation as to why he didn't have her paintings—after telling Janet he had them. He tossed around different ideas but they all smacked of cover-up. He had to take the "high road" by telling her the truth…how he'd taken her paintings to the New Falls dump as clutter, as junk. No, forget it. Best to fudge it, Charlie. You're a lawyer, you'll think of something.

****

His trial Monday morning was uneventful and his interviews after lunch adhered to the schedule he had set for himself: to quit no later than 3:00. At 3:10 he cut short the rant of a 42-year-old woman who wanted to divorce her husband and have him pay—she didn't say "with his life" but she was thinking it. They made an appointment for another meeting and, minutes after, Charlie told his secretary he was leaving for the day.

On Main Street cars were moving very slowly; there seemed to be some kind of tie-up at the intersection. Charlie turned onto Elm Street as a detour. He was nervous about telling Janet that her painting had "mysteriously disappeared." She might say she understood but it seemed unlikely. He felt that he'd become something of a hero to her by cherishing her art—the way her eyes had brightened, the sweetness of her lips on his face—and he had hoped to build on those feelings by asking her, when she came by to view her paintings, to have a drink with him—

Suddenly Charlie braked, then stopped altogether. A faded blue Toyota pickup was parked at the curb next to a well-known mini-warehouse of used items. Looking for something? Go to Stan's. Charlie pulled over. A door jingled when he opened it. A rough-looking guy with thick fingers and a faded green baseball cap on his head was examining old bottles in a cardboard box.

"Howdy," he said, looking up.

"How you doing today?" Charlie said.

"No complaints."

"You must be Stan."

"I have lots of names. That's one of them."

Lanterns hung from the ceiling, as did ice skates and old steel traps. Hand tools lay on dusty shelves. Hardly an open foot of space anywhere. Charlie looked casually around. And there, propped against the wall near the proprietor, were the paintings. And the broken easel.

JUNK ART

He let another minute go by. Then he said, "Those paintings there—how did you come by them, if I might ask."

"My son went to the landfill yesterday," Stan said. "Paintings lay next to the burn pile. Another ten minutes, they would've went up in flames."

"They for sale?"

"Everything you see is for sale. The shop's for sale."

"What do you want for them?"

"What are they worth to you?"

Once, not a nickel, Charlie thought. "I'll give you fifty dollars for all seven."

"That's mighty fine of you," Stan said, appraising an old bottle of Milk of Magnesia.

"Well?" Charlie said.

"These paintings are signed by the artist, take a look." He pointed to the lower right-hand corner of one of the canvases. "Janet Summersell."

"Signed or unsigned, who cares?" Charlie said.

Stan's teeth, badly stained, looked like peanuts with the skins on. "Come back day after tomorrow, they'll be gone."

"I'll give you two-hundred dollars," Charlie said.

The proprietor took an old Coke bottle out of the box and held it up to the light.

Charlie glanced at his watch. Quarter to four. He had to get home, set the paintings up, change out of his suit. "Look, I'll give you five-hundred dollars."

"You got fifteen hundred bucks, they're yours."

"Seven hundred and fifty."

"One thousand," Stan said. "Final offer. I'll throw in the easel."

****

Charlie propped the paintings against two walls in the loft. They were grimy, splattered with specks of dirt and dead insects, and, fetching a whiskbroom and a water-dampened cloth, he gave them each a careful brushing and cleaning. Then he went inside and washed up, put on a navy golf shirt and a pair of crisp khakis, and went out to the deck. At 4:20 Charlie had the notion that Janet was replaying an old scene, but then he heard the reassuring sound of a car's tires crunching driveway stones.

He went down the steps as Janet was getting out. "Charlie," she said. "I'm late, sorry."

"It's nothing. Welcome to your old house."

Janet smiled and they walked toward the garage, then up the stairs to the loft.

"Here they are," he said.

She looked at each of the canvases separately, stepping back a little, then to the side. She paused, gave her work a second viewing. "Well, I'm glad to see these," she said, "and thank you for keeping them, Charlie. They actually look cared for. But I can't use them. I was a different person back then, going through a difficult divorce. My pallet bore witness to my life—unclear, muddy."

"I'm sorry to hear you say that," Charlie said.

"They're dark. Do you see any light?"

"A lot of paintings are dark. Rembrandt painted dark paintings," Charlie said.

"Well, that's Rembrandt," Janet said with a little laugh. Then, "You're probably sick of seeing these around. Do with them as you like."

He was actually looking at the painting for the first time. Beneath their dark tones, he saw forms, images—a covered bridge, a ramshackle old barn, a mountain landscape. "Well, it was important that you look," he said.

"It was, definitely." She gave a glance at her wrist. "Charlie, I really have to run."

"Stay awhile, have a drink with me," he said.

"I'd love to, but I'm catching a ride to JFK in an hour."

He was crestfallen. "Well, it's been nice seeing you again, Janet."

"We'll have a drink, next time."

They went down the steps and out to her car. "I hope your show goes well," he said.

"I'll send you an invitation. Goodbye, Charlie." Janet came in, gave him an embrace, then slid behind the wheel and drove away.

Instead of going into the house, he went up the steps to the loft. For a good while he sat in the oak chair looking at the paintings. Several of them would fit nicely in his den. He'd get them framed.

NEW WATER

When I was eleven, my father told me there was nothing wrong with fishing and baseball but a boy my age should start developing "finer, more cultivated interests" as well. He had recently met a viola player retired after seven years with the Pittsburgh Symphony, who was now living in our town and seeking pupils in both viola and violin. His name was Nick Bonino and he was looking forward to meeting me, my father said, for an introductory lesson.

Three days later, on a May morning made for fishing, my father drove me to Mr. Bonino's. We parked in a shale driveway in front of a weathered, rambling house that sat among drooping hemlocks. It was the dreariest, gloomiest-looking place I'd ever seen. I was one unhappy kid.

Mr. Bonino met us at the door. He had thick dark hair, a big nose and heavy-lidded eyes. Shortly after introductions my father left, and Mr. Bonino led me into a large room that had a couple of tall windows in it, also a piano, several straight-backed chairs and music stands. We sat down and he asked me about school, what I enjoyed doing. I said I was in the sixth grade, played baseball and loved fishing.

I was surprised when he asked me what kind of fishing and where I fished.

"In the Ashokan Reservoir, mostly with live bait and also plugs," I said. "Last year I caught a fifteen-inch smallmouth on a Red-Eyed Wobbler."

"Bravo, Gus!" Mr. Bonino said. "Did you ever fly fish for trout?"

"No."

"After we have our lesson, I'll show you my rods."

"How many do you have?"

"Six."

My violin teacher has six fishing rods?

Mr. Bonino opened a black case and withdrew a violin. We talked about the strings, each had a letter. From low to high: G D A E. He showed me how to hold the violin, how to use the bow. Our lesson, basically, was good posture, how to sit with the violin, how to make the stroke. More than once he said, "No slouching, Gus. Instrument high, bow-arm up."

When we were done—it seemed forever—we sat for a while. He talked about practice, several times used the word "discipline." Then he said, "Your father wants you to take an interest in the arts. I'm all for it. Everyone should have an appreciation, a love of the arts. But never let anyone tell you, Gus, that casting a dry fly isn't an art. Done well, it's music, it's poetry."

Had I heard him correctly?

I followed my teacher across the room to a narrow door. Hanging on it on a wooden hanger was a vest the color of fallen leaves. It had eight or ten various-sized pockets, not flat pockets like you see on a shirt. These pockets came out an inch or so and were filled, as I imagined, with wondrous fly-fishing stuff. I reached up and touched the material.

"Nice, isn't it?" Mr. Bonino said.

"It's beautiful!"

"My daughter made it for me."

"Your daughter. Wow! Does she live around here?"

"No." Then he said, "She's no longer with us, Gus."

It took me a second to understand. "Gee, I'm sorry, Mr. Bonino."

He gave me an easy rap on the shoulder and opened the door to a room, small in comparison to the music room. But how much more exciting. It was like a different world, one I may have dreamed about. In a glass-fronted cabinet stood shiny aluminum tubes of varying lengths. A wood-framed net with a leather-wrapped handle hung from a peg on the side of the cabinet; on the other side was a wicker creel, also trimmed in leather. On a large table lay boxes of hooks, pieces of fur, spools of thread. Mr. Bonino explained the term "neck." It meant the side of a rooster's neck, with all the feathers—the hackle—so important for tying dry flies. He had twenty necks in a big box, naming a few—Rhode Island Reds, California Grays, Iowa Blues. Clamped to the edge of the table was a long-stemmed beaklike vise; in it was a small hook partially tied. Finished flies, by the hundreds, were in plastic boxes, each with a label on it—Quill Gordon, Royal Coachman, March Brown, Light Cahill, Blue Dun....

Mr. Bonino unscrewed the top of an aluminum tube and pulled out a cloth sleeve, removed two sections of bamboo and fitted them snuggly together. He made a small casting motion, eye on the tip. "This is my seven-foot Payne," he said, and put it in my hand.

I held the cork handle, overcome by the lightness, the feel of the rod, the pure joy of holding it.

"If you show me you've been practicing the violin, I'll throw in lessons on casting," Mr. Bonino said. "How does that sound to you, Gus?"

****

Twenty-two years later, I had a couple of rods myself—and a wife and a daughter and a job—and Nick and I went fishing on the days when his teaching book was empty and my schedule, as an instructor of writing at the local community college, permitted. Most of the time we would hit the better known streams and creeks in the county, but once or twice a season Nick would find "new water." Driving along a narrow country road he would feel an impulse to stop his car, get out, and "follow his nose." He smelled trout, and trudging through woods and fields he would come to a creek, sometimes only two or three yards across, shallow, except for the occasional pocket. "Gus, scrappy ten-inch natives!" he'd tell me that evening. And we'd set a date.

We were seeking his newest new water on a June afternoon, so remote a spot that Nick couldn't rightly recall where on County 7A he had originally stopped—somewhere just outside Washburn Corners, pop. 819. Near an old yellow barn, he said. Or was it red? In any event we stopped at an old barn and hiked on terrain that could serve as a Marine training camp, Nick every once in a while sniffing the air. And we came to a stream at last, so drooping with branches as it trickled along that fishing it was almost impossible. We couldn't resist the challenge. When we returned to my car an hour later, I had two 8-inch brook trout in my creel and Nick had one, a 10-inch beauty. We pulled apart our rods, took off our boots. I slipped off my vest and watched Nick remove his. It wasn't tattered but was showing wear, a lot of wear; in several places the material was so thin you could see the edge of a fly box or the leather pouch of a second reel.

Dusk was settling when we parked in front of his house among the hemlocks forty minutes later. He was limping; arthritis was acting up. I was feeling a few aches myself from the hike. Inside, hanging his vest on the narrow door, he asked me if I'd care for a glass of wine.

"Sure. Let me call Joan."

The phone lay on a low, round table in his den. A fireplace, constructed of football-sized fieldstones, took up one wall, and a bookshelf, filled with volumes on fly fishing, music, and the classics, filled another. It was a warm, comfortable room. I dialed my house and my 8-year-old daughter answered on the second ring.

"Hi, Ellie. We just got back," I said.

"How was it, Daddy?"

"Two little ones, good for breakfast. Tell Joan I'll be home in twenty minutes."

"My A string broke."

"I'll get one from Nick."

I hung up. Seeing a Herter's Catalog on the table, I picked it up; opening to an inserted envelope, I saw four or five different pictures of fly fishermen's vests. Just then Nick came in wearing a different shirt, a dark blue made of chamois cloth, carrying two glasses of red wine. He had washed up and combed his hair; it was still thick but mostly gray. He set the wine on the table and sat in an easy chair with a grimace. Picking up a glass he said, "Here's to you, Gus. Another season come and gone."

We touched glasses. "That's a nice little stream," I said. "But stop finding new water, Nick. It's killing us."

He had a good laugh; we both did.

"I see you're looking at vests," I said.

He picked up the catalog, glanced at the pictures, gave his head a shake. "Who designs these vests anyway? How could I ever buy one, Gus?"

The answer was very simple: he couldn't. We sat there, talking—it wasn't just, or always, about fly fishing and trout. I was writing a novel, and Nick was genuinely interested in it. And there were his reflections, memories of his boyhood in Rochester and the beatings his father would "administer" if he hadn't put in a full three hours daily on the viola. Trout fishing had saved his life—he'd told me more than once. We finished our wine.

"Give my love to Joan," he said.

"I will. Ellie just told me her A string had broken."

Nick got up, limped to his studio, and came back holding a square white envelope. "I'll see her on Wednesday. She's really coming along."

"I'm glad. Listen, Nick, I have an idea." I felt uneasy going ahead with it but I did anyway. "I'd like to take your vest home with me. The season's over so we have time. Joan's a great sewer and designer. She'd be happy to make a copy of your vest and you'd have it for next year."

He smiled. "That would be great, if she's up to it. Give me a minute to empty the pockets."

****

We were sitting in the living room with Ellie, and Joan was holding Nick's limp, worn vest. "When would he want it?"

"No rush. By next spring."

"No aspersions, it needs washing." She set the vest aside. "Why doesn't he simply *buy* a vest, Gus?"

"He says they aren't right—the length, the pocket design; but it's more than that."

"Didn't Angela make it for him?" Ellie said.

"She did, yes."

"Was it her pattern?" Joan asked.

"He told her what he wanted and she put it together; that's all he's ever said."

"Let me see how it goes," Joan said. "I'd love to do it for Nick."

She soaked the vest, then washed it by hand and put it on a hanger to dry. Joan was working on a children's book—writing the story and doing the illustrations—and with no deadline on the vest she let the project slide. In November we went into a fabric store in Kingsley-on-Hudson and picked out the finest, highest-count poplin available, a rich tan; and soon afterward Joan began making a pattern, following the exact measurements of the original. In early December she took scissors in hand. I was glad to see she was going about it in good spirits, with Ellie doing all she could to help—by not getting too much in her mother's way. With the cutting done, Joan started "assembling" the new vest. Feeling happy and excited, I wandered into her sewing room that evening. She was seated at her machine; looking on, at her elbow, was Ellie. I stood there for a moment, thinking Joan would smile and say something positive. She didn't even look up.

"How's it going?" I asked. No reply. "Can I get you anything, Joan?"

"No. Thanks."

My daughter gave me a nervous, confused look.

"Just poking my head in," I said. "See you."

I had a ton of college papers to correct and plowed into them for a couple of hours. At 10:15, I called it a day and found Joan in bed with a book. "How are you?" I asked.

"I'm not sure I'll be able to make the vest," she said.

"Joan, you're doing fine!"

"I'm not doing fine at all," she said.

I sat down on the edge of the bed. "OK. What's the problem?"

"I don't know."

"You're in there, working; you have to know what the problem is."

"I don't know what the problem is, Gus!"

"Well, maybe you're going too fast," I said. "Slow down."

"You don't understand," she said.

"That's true, I don't."

She went back to her book.

I didn't inquire about the vest for the next two days, not wanting to appear as if I were putting pressure on my wife; but on the third day, while doing clean-up after dinner, I heard shouts coming from her sewing room. I went in. Joan's hands were in her hair.

"What's the matter?" I asked.

"Nothing."

"Joan, something is the matter."

"She stitched one of the pockets wrong," Ellie said.

"You should be in bed, it's past your bedtime!" Joan snapped at her daughter.

Ellie left the room, holding back tears.

"Would you like a cup of tea?" I asked my wife. "A glass of wine? Anything?"

"Just leave me alone," she said.

I walked out. Ellie was washing up and I talked to her for a minute, saying I should have known better than to enlist her mother for the job. Ellie didn't say very much but I saw she was unhappy, and two days later she came into my office and told me that Mom was sitting at her sewing machine not doing anything, just kind of staring.

She was not, however, at her machine when Ellie and I walked in. The room was empty. Lying next to the old vest on the daybed, as if thrown there, was the new one, or that part of the new one that was finished. I held it up, looking at it closely. The front pockets were definitely wrong, the bellows effect extending only to the sides and not, as on the original, to the bottoms. Furthermore, the over-all shape was faulty, or appeared that way, though I couldn't determine exactly where, or how, the design differed. The upper left pocket was torn off, dangling by a thread, and there was a scissors cut—it seemed like a wound—in the material where the pocket belonged. I blew out a breath and let the vest—the vest that never was—drop to the daybed.

"Is she stopping?" Ellie asked.

"I'm afraid so."

"Daddy, I wanted to help her." She was crying.

"I know." I gave her a hug. "I know you did, Ellie."

A thin trail of smoke spiraled upward from the stone chimney of Nick's house several days later as I parked my car. He was in his den reading when I walked in. Looking up, he saw what I had in my hand.

"So, Gus," he said, standing, "how goes it?"

"Not so good."

I set the vest on a chair and we sat down at the round table. "Nick, I don't know what to say. We had the material, Joan made a pattern—she worked on it diligently. It just wouldn't turn out for her. She's really sorry. We all are."

He poured two glasses of wine. "Tell her I appreciate her efforts," he said.

"I will."

We were quiet for a while. Then Nick said, "Funny thing about that vest. Three winters ago—I don't know if I ever told you this—a pupil of mine told me she couldn't afford lessons any longer. Times were hard. Husband had lost his job. She loved the viola and wanted to continue studying. Now this woman, Gus, just happened to make slip covers and draperies professionally—so we worked out a deal. She'd make a new vest for me, copying it from the old, and I'd give her six free lessons—by then maybe her husband would have a job and she could start paying me again."

"What happened?"

"Her husband called me after two weeks and said Rosalie was having a nervous break-down and he'd drop off my god-damn vest in the morning!"

I sat there looking at him, part of me wanting to laugh; but I didn't laugh.

"I'm beginning to think—" Nick glanced at the vest draped over a chair, "—that it and I will turn to dust together."

The warmth of the fire felt good; its light flickered across his face. "Anyway," he said, "to more important matters. Ellie's last lesson with me was superb!"

"Are you saying she has more talent than I had, as a kid?"

Nick broke into laughter. "Gus, musical ability often skips a generation. Your old man was so-so, you were abysmal, and Ellie has a genuine gift."

When I got home I told my wife and daughter that Nick had taken the matter of the vest philosophically. Joan was glad to hear it, but Ellie still seemed upset, as if we—or maybe she—had somehow failed her teacher and friend. Perhaps it was only my imagination but shortly afterward, as she was practicing her little airs, I detected a sadness in her music which I had never noticed before.

January passed, cold, dark; February, the same. For several days Nick fought a bad chest inflammation and fever; but a fisherman is lucky, because his blood starts warming long before the weather. "Gus," he said to me over the phone in early March, "come on over tonight. We'll leaf through the new Herter's. I need a creel harness and some felt soles for my waders. Bring over a list and we'll place an order."

Opening Day came, but Nick and I didn't go out. We waited, as was our custom, for the first fly of the season, of significance to the angler, to appear on the stream, usually during the third week in April. That was *Iron Fraudator* (its imitation, the Quill Gordon). The fly always emerged in the early afternoon, and at one sharp on April 24th Nick and I pulled off the road, near one of our favorite early-season streams, and began putting on our gear. Nick looked thin after the long winter, physically depleted, and my heart ached when he slipped into his old vest, now, of certainty, facing its last season. We assembled our rods and began walking toward the water.

Spring gave way to summer. Likewise *Iron Fraudator* to *Ephemerella Subvaria*—the Hendrickson; to *Stenonema Vicarium*—the March Brown; to *Stenonema Canadensis*—the Light Cahill; to *Isonychia Bicolor*—the Dun Variant. The season continued, the streams became low, very clear, both of us now using 12-foot leaders tapered to 5x. In late September, our flies floated on lazy currents, sometimes nudged aside by little regattas, sails of yellow and red and orange.

And so it was the following year...and the years following. As for Nick's vest, I'd obviously misjudged the life it still had in it. Perhaps it would hold up forever, or in any case as long as the man who wore it. He and it might, indeed, turn to dust together.

Meanwhile, my daughter continued her studies with Nick. Ellie's was a fine talent, in his judgment; she was a gifted young violinist and could become, with time and practice, a truly accomplished musician. She was not a sad child but a quality of sadness, which I had sensed years before, still issued from her bow. Frequently when I would call for her at the conclusion of her lesson, I would sit and listen to her play for the last five minutes; and, listening, would find myself casting a fly on an autumn stream, alone. No doubt my reveries were helped along by the old, old vest on the narrow door.

Looking over at it, one mid-winter afternoon while listening to Ellie play, I saw it wasn't there. The hanger was empty, and I knew someone else was trying to do what others had tried to do. Nick's hip was bothering him; his eyes were darkly circled, he was fighting his yearly chest ailment, and I could only hope that whoever the individual was, she or he would succeed. Ten days before the trout season opened, the old vest was back on its hanger, barely holding on.

We continued fishing together but each season less and less; then one spring Nick missed the entire hatch of *Iron Fraudator*, a stretch of some two weeks. It was as unlikely as the Pope's letting the Easter season come and go without celebrating it. I began fishing alone, more and more, and often as I worked an evening hatch or sat on the tailgate of my station wagon with four or five trout in my creel, the rushing of a near-by stream filling the summer night, I would think, Nick Bonino, where are you? Sometimes, if it wasn't too late, I would stop by his place to give him a report on the day's hatch, what flies were emerging, the conditions of the water; but often I would park my car and not go into his house at all, because through the drooping hemlocks the strains of his viola would reach my ear, mournful, solitary, sadder even than an autumn stream with leaves floating by.

Ellie kept at her lessons, so I saw Nick regularly even though we fished together rarely. She became a young woman, and on Nick's urging, as she advanced both musically and scholastically, she applied to Julliard. She looked very lovely at her high school graduation in a cool violet gown she had designed and her mother had made. She was introduced by the principal. First she played a selection from Schumann, then Ravel. Nick was with us in the auditorium, and he listened proudly. I think he loved our daughter as much as we did. All that summer she studied with him, then left for school in the early fall.

I didn't see Nick until mid-November in the village hardware store where he was buying some insulating strips for his windows. Naturally we spoke about Ellie. He was missing her, he said. As we walked out of the store together, he told me he had just lost a student and would be losing another at the end of the month. He was limping badly; as never before, he said, he dreaded the thought of winter. Saying goodbye to him on the sidewalk, I did too.

We had our first snowfall in late November and the snow stayed because the weather turned immediately cold. I called Nick, stopped by unannounced on a couple of occasions, and on another occasion he came for dinner. Ellie returned for the Christmas holiday, and after visiting with Nick one evening she came home and said they had played duets for violin and viola and had talked about her life. He couldn't have been warmer, she told us, but something was gone, something was missing in his life. Nick had told her he hadn't tied a fly in years.

"He hasn't cast a fly in years," I said.

The winter really set in after New Year's, and toward the end of January Nick took ill. He was laid up for three weeks, and while no further student had left him he was clearly scraping by. Joan prepared him frequent dishes which I brought over; then I would stay, hoping to revive his spirits with fisherman's talk: the famous hatches we had witnessed on the Beaverkill, the Schoharie, the East Branch, when we might have thought storm clouds had suddenly moved in, so dark with insects the sky. By mid-February he was up and around, giving lessons again, but he moved very slowly. He asked me, one afternoon, if I would like a glass of wine. Fine, I said, but he should sit—I would get it. I went to the pine cabinet near Nick's studio entrance. His vest, hanging in its old place, was thin as a mist at dawn; and painful as it was to accept, at that moment I had to accept that my old friend, who could smell a trout a half-mile away, had simply given up the quest.

Somehow winter ended, and in mid-March I found myself going over my gear, deciding what I'd need for the coming season. Definitely a new line. As I was flipping through my outfitters' catalogs, I suddenly stopped. Nick was the proudest man I knew and I didn't want to insult him. Then I thought every other fly fisherman in America wears and uses these vests, and I would like to buy him the nicest one on the market and include a note, "Who could forge a second Excalibur, recreate the Mona Lisa? Wear this in health, and meet me on the stream damn-it-to-hell!" Or something like that. But I didn't fill out the order. I couldn't do it.

Ellie came home for spring recess and we invited Nick for dinner. When he knocked on our door, she opened it, and for a long moment they held each other. Then we sat around the fire, talking. The strenuous winter was over, but Nick was still feeling the effects of it—you could see it in his face, hear it in his voice. In years past, as fishing season approached, a portion of the conversation would have involved fishing, but it was only mentioned once—when I told Nick I'd bought myself a new floating line. He mentioned the old-style line that fly fishermen would have to dress routinely to keep from sinking and I said I remembered well; he'd given me one when I was thirteen. Nick said he'd wanted to get me started right. Joan served a fine dinner and afterward, at Nick's request, Ellie played her violin. I saw the joy in his dark eyes as she performed, and I could almost hear him saying, "That's the stroke right there, Gus. Fly fishing and the violin! Poetry, music!"

He clapped and said, "Bravo!" Then we all sat together in front of the fire and drank coffee, talked for a while. Nick praised Ellie's performance once again and said he should be going. He had a student coming at eight o'clock in the morning before reporting to her job.

Without saying a word Ellie left the room and returned with a handsomely wrapped box, blue paper and a forest-green ribbon, and handed it to Nick. He said something to the effect that it wasn't his birthday, or it wasn't Christmas—what was going on? I was thinking the same thing. Nick opened the box carefully, pushed aside the tissue paper—and said nothing. For a long while. Then he reached in and pulled out a fly-fisherman's vest, a replica, to the stag buttons, of the one his daughter had made him so many years ago.

"Thank you, Ellie."

"Try it on," Joan said.

"Not necessary," Nick said, fighting back tears. "I know it fits."

He kissed Ellie's cheek, said a quiet thank you to me and Joan, and left the house. We both flew on our daughter. When? How? Where?

"Our house mother has a sewing machine," she said. "I worked on it nights, Sundays. I found time."

"But the old vest is at Nick's," I said.

"I didn't need the old vest," Ellie said. "After all those years of seeing it on his door, I knew it by heart."

****

Not long after, on an evening in early May, the telephone rang in my house. I picked up, delighted to hear Nick's voice. "Gus, how are you for tomorrow?"

"I'll be back from the college about two. What's up?"

"I was in Lynwood Falls Monday checking on a small fiddle for one of my young pupils," he said, "and driving back on old Rt. 117, I had this feeling. Was my old nose telling me something? I parked and made my way through some scrubby-looking pines."

"And?"

"It's pretty water, Gus," he said. "You'll like it."

THE INTERMEDIATE SKIER

"That's Manuel Fortez!"

"Where?"

"There, in the blue jumpsuit, with the white stripe on the leg."

Glancing down, Jack spotted the man Eileen had just pointed out. Because he was descending so swiftly, and because Jack and Eileen were on the lift moving in the opposite direction, Jack barely managed a glimpse of the man's face; but even in that moment he recognized the dark, brutally handsome look he had always imagined Manuel Fortez to have.

"He skis well."

"He grew up in Switzerland," Eileen said.

"I thought he was a Spaniard."

"His father was a famous matador. His mother was Swiss."

They passed abreast of one of the steel towers rising at intervals to the top of Blue Mountain. The support arm, which connected their double-chair to the cable, click-clacked over the large revolving wheel attached to the tower's side.

"So, who else is at Blue Run today, of interest?" Jack inquired.

She didn't reply to his sarcasm. Soon they were approaching another tower. Wired to one of the cross-struts was a red-lettered sign: INTERMEDIATE SKIERS--PREPARE TO UNLOAD. As they drew near the station, approximately halfway to the top of the mountain, Jack and Eileen opened their safety bars.

A man smoking a pipe and wearing an orange hunting jacket momentarily detained their chair as it swept through—Eileen coasted off to the left, Jack to the right. At the crest of the intermediate slope they merged. It was their eighth run; they had already decided to take a break for lunch on finishing it. Far below, in the valley, the steeple of a church glowed brightly in the noon sun.

"Jack, I didn't point Manuel out to upset you," she said.

"I'm sure you didn't."

"Maybe it was insensitive of me, but after all this time I would think you'd get over it."

"I'd think so too."

He pushed off, skiing strongly but awkwardly, coming to a rough stop some hundred yards down the slope. That Fortez was at Blue Run would probably preoccupy him all day, and he was angry at her for having pointed him out— as if he and Manuel were pals! Trying to control his emotions, he watched Eileen come toward him in her slow but graceful way, traversing the hill. She was wearing a silver-fox hat, pale-gray stretch pants, and a red jacket….

He remembered the night eight years ago. They'd gone to a party, had had a pretty good time, but coming home she told him, sharply, that he'd spent too much time with "that willowy blonde." They'd had words, a typical first-year-of-marriage flare-up, over and forgotten in ten minutes. Except Eileen, instead of getting out of the taxi with him in old Chelsea, continued on, returning the following morning at 10:00—she'd slept at a girlfriend's, she said. He didn't believe her. For a week he steamed, accusing her of spending the night with her old lover, an artist named Manuel Fortez. She didn't change her story, even telling him he could call up Julie Barnett "for verification." Eventually he had seen the futility of it, and had let it drop. His law-school finals were coming up and he had to get down to some serious studying.

Clearly—Eileen was coming to an easy stop ten feet away— he hadn't let it drop at all.

"How are my turns looking?" she asked, as if nothing had occurred.

"Very nice. Excellent."

"I think I'm finally getting it, Jack."

They had a picnic-style lunch in the rustic cafeteria of the main lodge. Eileen had taken off her jacket and hat, and every now and then as they ate their sandwiches and salad she would glance at the entrance. Jack didn't say anything. She might have done it anyway; but he kept having the uncomfortable feeling that she was waiting for Manuel to walk in. If he did, chances were he'd recognize her and come over, and Jack wasn't at all that sure what he'd say or do. For the first four months after meeting Eileen, he'd felt himself in keen competition with her "artist friend in the Village," and not too positive he was holding his own. The man had international friends, a house in the Hamptons and a snappy car, and was always taking Eileen to the hottest clubs. Unhappy with the situation, wanting to settle it once and for all, Jack gave her an ultimatum. To his joy and great relief, Eileen broke off with the artist. Three months later she and Jack were married.

When they finished lunch they went back outside, finding their equipment amidst a mass of skis and poles leaning against a huge rack. On their second run of the afternoon, they became separated. It happened every time they skied. Blue Run was a large and popular resort, and with big weekend crowds and many different trails and crossovers, staying together all day, though not impossible, was unlikely. To ski alone for an hour or so, in fact, was something they both enjoyed, though it was never actually planned.

Jack took his place on the end of the lift line, three loops of skiers long. Unlike previous separations at Blue Run, however, he found himself glancing around looking for his wife. Didn't see her. He shuffled along. Two loops left. Didn't see her, Shuffle. One loop—

"Single!" barked the lift attendant.

"Here!" Jack yelled in response.

He pushed past three or four "twosomes" to join the other single on the lift.

The double-chair swept around the base tower, the attendant, in a green vest, detained it momentarily, and Jack and his companion sat, pulled shut their safety bars, and were on their way. The woman was in her late thirties, a buyer for a Brooklyn-based fabrics outlet, and a talker, and as she talked she appeared to observe—more in judgment than sympathy—Jack's outmoded skis, poles and boots.

"What do you do?" she asked, as they neared the station.

"I'm a lawyer."

"Really?"

Jack skied one of the more remote trails down, taking a crossover halfway to the bottom and emerging on another trail, looking around all the while—then was again waiting in line.

"Single!"

"Here!" Jack replied.

His companion was a dour, heavy-set individual who chose to keep to himself, and after a downhill that brought Jack anything but joy, he once again was in the lift line, thinking to take one more run before checking the lodge bar where (he was now convinced) she and Manuel were having a drink. This time Jack was the individual held aside by the attendant, who made his usual request: "Single!"

"Yo!" a man yodeled. Coasting up to Jack, he asked, "The left side or the right—do you have a preference?"

Jack didn't, but he was too shocked to reply.

"Then I will take the left," the man said, gliding gracefully into position.

"You gettin' on?" the attendant asked Jack.

Snapping out of his trance, he lunged forward as the chair passed through, just making it.

"So," said the man in blue, a single white stripe down the leg, "what a glorious day we have!"

"It is, yes."

"The conditions are superb, are they not? Blue Run is not world-class but I am always impressed with the challenges it presents, and how well it is groomed."

"It's a good area," Jack said, slowly collecting himself, recognizing the opportunity fate had handed him.

"Are you a native of these parts?" Manuel Fortez asked.

"I live in Lynwood, nearby."

"I have passed through. It is a lovely village."

Fortez's skis were a rich brown graphite; his poles had zigzag shafts and his boots, handsomely molded, had quick-action snaps. They passed a steel tower. Click-clack.

"You must ski Blue Run frequently, living so close. No?"

"Occasionally," Jack said. "How about you?"

Fortez wore a dazzling white band around his head, covering his ears. His hair was dark and thick, beginning to gray at the sides. His skin glistened, as if he had just applied a fine lotion or emollient. Hovering in or around the chair was a subtle masculine scent. He said, "Maybe twice a season you will find me here, but I am usually at more renowned areas. Just this past week I have returned from Chamonix. Ah, yes!"

What the "Ah, yes!" signified, Jack couldn't rightly say. Perhaps it was an exclamation of praise for Chamonix; or possibly for the woman in pink, with flying dark hair, who at that moment was passing beneath the lift. Fortez's head turned as she continued down the trail.

"If you have just come from Chamonix," Jack said, "this must be very tame for you—maybe boring."

"These are not the Alps to be sure," Fortez said, his attention returning to the slope. "But one does not ski for skiing alone." He paused. Then: "Magnifique!"

"Excuse me?"

"There, in the lavender. That one has the knowledge."

"The knowledge?"

"A certain *je ne sais quoi.*" Fortez came back to an earlier comment. "No, never for skiing alone! And I will tell you, even in Chamonix the après-ski is not so fine as here!"

Click-clack.

Fortez's eagle eyes remained on the hillside. "The young one in green skiing so cautiously? Do you see her? That is *entre les deux.*"

"You'll have to explain."

"No longer a girl, not quite a woman. They hunger to learn."

They were now more than halfway to the intermediate station, Jack's point of departure. Fortez, of course, would continue to the top. Time was running out. To keep the dialogue going, he asked Fortez where he lived.

"Six months out of the year I have a place in Greenwich Village," Fortez said. "The rest of the year I move about—mostly abroad. In August I am usually in the Hamptons or—" His voice trailed off. "Ah, yes. There is the knowledge, my friend. That is the knowledge supreme!" Fortez strained for a closer look. "But wait! This one I know!"

Jack looked down. More on Fortez's side of the slope than his, resting on her poles in a triangle of sunlight, was Eileen.

"C'est incroyable!" said Fortez.

"What is?" Jack inquired.

"Seeing her. That she is here."

"Who?"

"A past love. More than a love—a life!"

"Long ago?"

INTERMEDIATE SKIERS--PREPARE TO UNLOAD.

Jack's hand gripped the safety bar.

"It was not yesterday, not last year. It goes back," Fortez said. "I almost have her name. Eleanor? Louise? L—it is a name with an L."

ANTHONY ROBINSON

They were entering the leveled-off area; just beyond, the expert trail began rising, climbing precipitously to the top of Blue Run. "Lily? How can I forget, when we were so close, so passionately in love?"

The chair swept through. "Mon Dieu!" Fortez cried out, upset with himself, "why did I not get off? But no difference. Soon I shall be flying to her side!"

"How—how do you know she's not spoken for?"

"Is that a problem? To me, it is a challenge. But it returns—it is coming back—even as to when we met!"

Click-clack.

"It was on the beach, I had a summer house on Fire Island—in a black bikini, she was. I introduced myself. My reputation as an artist was growing, she knew me, had seen my work. 'But I must paint you,' I implored. 'Come to my studio in the morning.' To my delight, she appeared. As I put charcoal to paper, my hand shook! My vision blurred!"

"Was she naked?"

"Was I interested in her clothing?" Fortez smiled. "I have seen the bodies of many beautiful women, but hers—hers was nonpareil! On a break we sipped tea, we talked. Then we made love."

"That—that same morning?"

"For the better part of a year, we were together. She would come to my Greenwich Village loft—half Mona Lisa, half tiger! I never painted so well, made love with such abandon. It was the only period of my whole life that I stayed faithful to one woman. Oh, the knowledge she had, the immense, boundless knowledge! Eloise? Lorraine? Help me, my friend."

"Eileen."

"But that is it! Yes, Eileen!"

Click-clack.

"What happened to her?"

"Like most women she wanted a family, young ones. I weakened, I listened to my heart. How close I came to taking her for my wife! But the artist in me won out. I wasn't cut out to be a husband, a father. It ended our relationship. She met someone else—yes, yes, I am seeing it all. A 'boy' she kept calling him. The boy would give her a home and children. She did not love him. How many times would she lie in my arms and cry! He was a struggling student, I remember so vividly. And finally, one evening, we parted. How we both wept! We had an all-consuming love. I have never known anything like it since, and likely never will again."

Click-clack.

Jack hazarded a glance over his shoulder at the steep drop. Shaking off a sharp attack of vertigo, he asked the question he had to ask. "After she and the 'boy' got married, did—did you ever see her again?"

"After she left, I wandered, lost, it was a terrible time. The emptiness of my life!" Fortez said. "Then one night, a year to a year and a half had passed, there came a knock. It awakened me, and when I opened the door to my loft I could only think I was dreaming. It was Eileen! She had just had a fight with her husband, she said. She was more attractive, more beautiful than ever! We began kissing. Until the break of dawn, we made love. If I had died the next day, I would have died a happy man."

Fortez lifted his face to the breeze coming off the top of Blue Run; he was smiling; for a moment his eyes closed. "When we awoke later that morning," he said, as if coming to, "I beseeched her to leave the boy. We would get married immediately—we'd fly to Mexico!—we could even have a child! Alas, it was then she told me she was already pregnant and felt—how shall we call it?—an obligation. An obligation! What is an 'obligation' compared to love? But she left; for the second time we bid each other farewell. I remember the last words she spoke. 'Maybe one day again, Manuel.'"

EXPERT SKIERS--PREPARE TO UNLOAD.

"And perhaps, my friend, that day has come!"

Fortez threw open his safety bar, skied off as the double-chair swept through the station, and glided to the edge. Jack lurched after him, almost spilling. "There's something you should know," he said.

"Something I should know?"

"You—you have been talking about my wife," Jack said, next to Fortez on the summit of Blue Run. A great snow-covered countryside stretched out below them.

"Ah, you are a clever one—you would like to meet her yourself, no? Ha-ha!"

"Stay away from her. Do you understand me?"

Two teen-aged boys, in blue jeans, skied off the lift and plunged over the edge like sky-divers. "I'll tell you what," Fortez said. "We shall race. Is that not fair? As the whole world knows—ha-ha!—the prize goes to the swift!"

He gave Jack a little smile of contempt. "Adieu, et bon chance!" he said, and pushed off.

On impulse, Jack thrust his right pole out and snagged the tip of the artist's ski with its saucer-sized basket. Fortez did a complete flip, landing with a tremendous crash on the hard-packed surface, head first. Then he slid, bounced, rolled down the treacherous incline, both skis tearing loose from his boots, at last coming to rest in a straggle of pines just off the trail.

Jack gave a quick glance around, to see who might've noticed. A skinny, horse-faced woman in black pants and a fifty-year-old man with a reddish-gray beard were just leaving the chair. They glided over and peered down the steeply pitched slope to the person lying motionless some eighty yards away. The bearded man turned to Jack and asked him what had happened.

"He—he seemed to catch a tip and went head over heels. It was all so sudden."

"We'd better alert the ski patrol," the bearded man said.

He whistled to the lift attendant, who left his post, took a look, and returned to his station where he picked up a phone. Within minutes several skiers were surrounding Fortez, and ten or more stood with Jack at the top, looking down. Three members of the ski patrol in rust-colored parkas and green armbands arrived. They lifted Fortez carefully, placed him on the cushion of a toboggan-like stretcher and strapped him in. One of the ski patrol took a position in front of the toboggan; another patrol member stood behind it. Snowplowing, they started down the mountain. When the rescue team disappeared, Jack pushed over to the station.

The attendant had a lined and leathery face. He glanced up. "Yes?"

"Is there an alternative trail to the bottom," Jack asked, "something not so steep?"

The man pointed off to his left, through a thick stand of hemlocks. "Follow the signs for 'Deer Path.' It runs along the crown, then circles in." He made a sweeping motion with his arm.

"Thanks."

Jack skied the long moderately pitched trail in no rush to get to the bottom. When he did, he saw an ambulance just leaving the main parking lot. He took off his skis, thinking to look for Eileen in the lodge, when he spotted her among a small crowd of observers. She looked very distressed. He walked over to meet her.

"Jack—something terrible happened," she said, her eyes tearing.

"What?"

"I was waiting in line when the ski patrol came by with a toboggan. Of all people, Manuel Fortez was on it."

"How is he?"

She bowed her head, grimacing. "I heard the patrol talking with the ambulance crew. He'd taken a terrible spill, he'd broken his neck."

"My goodness."

"He's dead."

Jack said nothing.

"No one knows how it could've happened," Eileen said. "I didn't want to see Manuel. I was hoping we wouldn't bump into each other. But this—it's so difficult to believe."

"I know."

They were standing as close to each other as their skis would allow. "Jack, I want to tell you something. Maybe because of what just happened."

"It's not necessary," he said quietly.

"I was a spoiled, shallow, impressionable girl—"

82

"It's all right, Eileen."

"I'd like to go home," she said.

"Let me get my skies."

Jack returned to the rack. The basket on one of his poles was bent, elongated. His eyes went to the mountain, to the ribbon of double-chairs stretching to the top of Blue Run. *Click-clack.* Taking a deep breath, he hoisted his skis and poles to his shoulder and walked back to where his wife was waiting.

BLOWING TUBES

It was almost noon when Lieutenant (junior grade) Andrew Sansevere stepped onto the bridge of the USS *Lawrence.* Mitch Price, also a junior-grade lieutenant, came out of the pilothouse to greet him on the starboard wing.

"Andy, prepare to be bored," he said. "Absolutely nothing is going on. We're on course zero-nine zero at twelve knots. The *Hunold, Ylvisaker,* and *Raymond* are astern in a single column— distance between ships 1000 yards. Nothing on the radar. Nothing on the books, no division exercises planned. Just plain old steaming. Captain Krist is in his sea cabin. At our present speed, you'll be able to see the California coast at 15:00."

"I relieve you," Andy said.

"I stand relieved."

They exchanged easy salutes. Price lifted the binoculars over his head and handed them over, then announced to the pilothouse crew, "Mr. Sansevere is now officer of the deck."

The sailors acknowledged and Price went below. Andy made a slow sweep of the horizon, then walked to the rear of the bridge and viewed the column of DD's that comprised Destroyer Division 271—homeward bound after a seven-month tour in wartime waters off North Korea, on the Formosa Patrol, on plane-guard duty with Task Force 77. He moved past the flag locker to the port side, walked through the pilothouse chatting with the sailors and came out on the starboard wing. In three hours, as California peeked over the horizon, cheers would go up on the *Lawrence.* Andy's fiancée would be among the throng waiting for the division to pull in. He could picture Nicole on the pier, waving happily, her copper-blond hair shining in the sun.

Andy checked the radar screen on the ship's starboard binnacle. So much to think about, to talk over. In ten days his three years' mandatory service in the navy reserves would be over. He could work with Nicole's father, Winston J. Hammer, a big-time realtor in Manhattan, or commit to the navy—drop the R out of USNR—and sign on as a career officer.

At this hour, as they were nearing home, Andy didn't know what career path to choose. Winston Hammer had no children besides Nicole, whom he dearly loved, and was offering the couple the keys to the store. Among the perks was a rent-free duplex apartment on East 64th Street. Andy stood to walk into a lot of money, luxury, travel; but the politics, the idea of working for his wife's father, didn't sit with him well. His love was the navy. His father, a writer, had served as an enlisted man during WWII and the stories he'd told Andy about the sea, about shipboard life, had stayed with him all his days. Andy was pretty sure that Nicole, naturally enough, would like him to join her father. A life as a navy wife wasn't out for her, but clearly wasn't what she preferred. In a recent letter to her, he had said he was "leaning navy," and she replied that it wasn't what she had hoped to hear him say. Between the lines he'd read that she was hoping he'd come to his senses.

Andy lifted the binoculars and scanned the horizon. Twice he circled the bridge and from time to time searched the ocean, near and far. A quiet watch. Plenty of time to think. Then the bridge phone talker, who followed the OOD around as his mouthpiece, was saying, "Mr. Sansevere, engine room requests permission to blow tubes."

Carbon and soot, building up in the ship's oil-fed power plant, worked against steaming efficiency; therefore, on average once a day, a request to "scrub the system" reached the bridge. Permission was necessary because blowing tubes sent up a whole lot of thick black smoke roaring through the stacks. Wanting to size up the situation before responding, Andy went to the rear of the bridge where he glanced overhead at the flag, observed the direction of the waves coming in, took into account the division's easterly course, and came to the less-than-scientific but well-considered judgment that the *Hunold,* next astern, might get a showering of soot on her decks.

"Not granted," Andy said to Rodriguez, who relayed the message to the engine room.

Moments later the phone talker was saying into his mouthpiece, as if answering a question, "Mr. Sansevere."

"What was that about?" Andy asked the sailor.

"Engine room wanted to know who had the deck."

As if the *name* of the OOD had any bearing. He, Andy Sansevere, hadn't said, "Not granted." The officer of the deck had said it, and only the captain and executive officer had greater authority on board ship. Andy gave his head an annoyed shake, knowing full well who had made the inquiry. Brendan Cartwright, the engineering officer.

Heavy footsteps hurriedly mounting the bridge ladder caught Andy's attention. The next moment Cartwright, all six-feet-two and 225 pounds of him, barged onto the wing. His meaty face damp with sweat, he went up to Andy.

"What do you mean, 'not granted?'"

"Conditions aren't right," Andy said.

"Who says?"

"I say."

"Right, the OOD," he said, chortling.

He was from Dallas, had gone to Texas A&M, and from the beginning, when he'd come on board two years ago, he and Andy had had little to say to each other. Andy was willing to put out his hand but Cartwright wanted no part of a truce. He was scornful of Andy's Ivy League background and had a mean, domineering way. Even now, as the officer of the desk, Andy felt threatened.

"We're in contention with the *Ylvisaker* for an 'E' in fuel conservation, if you didn't know," he said, looking down at Andy. "If we don't blow tubes, we're done."

"We'd likely dump soot on the *Hunold,*" Andy said.

"Bullshit! Have your talker call the engine room—"

"Brandon, you're out of line," Andy said, his heart pounding. "I'm ordering you off the bridge."

"Fuck you, Sansevere. Blow tubes!"

"Get your goddamn ass off this bridge, Cartwright!" Andy shouted, hands tightening, color rising to his face.

From the pilothouse doorway: "Mr. Sansevere!"

Andy glanced over. It was Captain Krist. "Sir?"

"I'm relieving you as officer of the deck."

"Captain, I don't understand."

"You are relieved, Mr. Sansevere."

He left the bridge in a daze. In his stateroom in officers' country, Andy sat at the little built-in desk trying to get hold of what had just happened. Why had the captain ordered him off the bridge when Cartwright was clearly in the wrong? It didn't make sense. He was sitting with his head in his hands when there was a knock outside his curtain.

"Yes?"

The boatswain's mate of the watch looked in. "The captain wants to see you in his stateroom, sir."

Andy rinsed and dried his face, put on his hat, and went up one flight to the main deck. He knocked at the captain's door, waited for a formal "Enter," and went in.

Captain Krist's stateroom, three times the size of a junior officer's, had its own porthole, a full carpet on the deck, and a large aluminum wardrobe against the bulkhead. The commanding officer was at his desk. "What do you have to say for yourself, Mr. Sansevere?"

Andy didn't stand at attention but he wasn't relaxed, far from it. "The engine room requested permission to blow tubes," he said. "After sizing up the waves, the wind direction, the colors aloft, I judge the *Hunold* might get hit. I say to my talker, 'Not granted.' In two minutes Mr. Cartwright storms the bridge and starts yelling. I tell him we're not blowing tubes because the *Hunold* might get hit. He says, 'Bullshit!' and insists I call the engine room. I tell him to leave the bridge and he doesn't go. He uses abusive language. I repeat the order and next thing I know you've relieved me of the watch."

Captain Krist, a Naval Academy graduate, opened a manila folder on his desk. The *Lawrence* was his first command of a combatant ship. He never smiled. He had an overshot lower jaw that looked like a scupper. "I have a memo here," he said, and began reading. "'Lieutenant (junior grade) Andrew Sansevere, USNR, has it firmly in mind to go USN. I am pleased by his intentions. As the *Lawrence's* gunnery officer Mr. Sansevere brought great credit to the ship. He received a Bronze Star for courage under fire in shelling and destroying a freight train on the mainland of North Korea.'"

Captain Krist closed the folder. "I will write that in your fitness report due next week." He looked at Andy directly. "But I will also say you were relieved as officer of the deck on this date. For a minor incident, but for me it says everything. You failed in the most important characteristics a navy officer can have—*patience, self-control, clear-headedness.* You handled the situation with Mr. Cartwright very badly. The bridge of a navy ship is not a schoolyard where you duke it out! Your fists were clenched—you were ready to go at it with Mr. Cartwright. As the OOD, you were responsible for two-hundred and thirty-three men and a navy ship. That it was an easy-going watch is no excuse. You let yourself get drawn in; your ego was on the line. When Mr. Cartwright became unruly, a distraction, you should have told the boatswain's mate of the watch, 'Captain to the bridge!' and walked away. But no, you had to have it out with a hot-headed junior officer. You can still go USN but the Officer Promotion Committee in D.C. is only too ready to shoot a candidate down. I was passed over twice for commander, for reasons less egregious than being relieved as an OOD. What happened just now is no way to start a career as a naval officer, Mr. Sansevere. It would dog you at every turn." Captain Krist folded his long, thin arms across his chest. "Do you have anything to say?"

He almost said, "No, sir," but Andy caught himself. Something was on his mind and he felt compelled to speak. "I was wrong arguing with Mr. Cartwright," he began. "Whether I go regular or leave the service, it was a lesson learned. As for why I told the engine room 'Not granted.' Was I going to let soot fall on the *Hunold,* after all we'd been through these past months? Mr. Cartwright didn't see it that way. His only concern is winning the division Excellence Award. Winning it would look great for the *Lawrence,* I understand; but at the expense of her good will by raining soot on the *Hunold?* Not on my watch. We're the lead ship and we can do better than that. Even if it means losing the E."

Captain Krist gave the junior-grade lieutenant a slow look. "You may leave, Mr. Sansevere."

"Thank you, Captain."

In the passageway, Andy passed through an open bulkhead door, stepped out to the main deck and walked aft. Sailors were busy polishing the brightwork, getting the ship ready for homecoming. At the depth-charge racks on the fantail, Andy stopped, taking in the light-gray line of DD's steaming gracefully along. What had made him think he was cut out for a navy career? The captain was right. He didn't have it in him to be a commanding officer. Leaders didn't lose their cool when confronted by the Brendan Cartwrights; they stood firm. Andy dipped his head, overcome with uncertainty. The next moment a deep roaring, as of a whirlwind, filled the air. He turned, looked upward. The ship's twin stacks were belching heavy black smoke. He watched as the noxious cloud drifted aft, veering south just in time and missing the *Hunold.*

Of that he was glad. He began walking forward. The hell with the navy. Later today he would say to Nicole there was no way he would work for her father. Andy Sansevere didn't know what he wanted to do with his life, but that wasn't it.

THE CANDIDATE

Wilson Sumrall walked from the kitchen of his house into the front hall. Looking up the blue-carpeted stairs, he shouted, "Lewis, rise and shine!"

He waited for a reply. When none came, he called again, louder. "Lewis, get up! We have a long way to go today!"

A garbled response drifted down, and Sumrall padded back to the kitchen in old leather slippers and a forest-green robe. As he was buttering toast, a boy of fourteen came in wearing pajama bottoms and a T-shirt and sat down at the table.

"Good morning," said Sumrall.

"G'morning."

Sumrall set two plates of scrambled eggs on the table and pulled out a chair. After a minute he said, "Nervous?"

The boy yawned. He had thick, dark-brown hair and large hazel eyes, still puffy with sleep. "No. Should I be nervous?"

"I thought you might be, that's all."

"It's just talking to people. What's the big deal?"

"Lewis," Sumrall said, irritated by his son's cavalier attitude, "conceivably, just *conceivably*, you could be nervous!"

"No sweat, Dad."

Sumrall gave his head a frustrated shake, sipped his coffee. "What are you going to wear?"

"My corduroy jacket and brown pants."

"With a tie—no open shirt!"

After breakfast, Sumrall went into his room and chose clothes for himself: a pair of easy-fitting flannel trousers, a gray-herring-bone sports jacket, and a blue shirt and necktie. In ten minutes he was again calling up to his son. "How're you doing?"

"All set."

The boy came down the stairs and Sumrall looked him over. "Fine—you look fine. But take off the Reeboks."

"Why?"

"A young man does not go to an interview in sneakers!"

"Dad, everyone--"

"Put on a pair of shoes, Lewis!"

The boy went back to his room. Sumrall waited, glancing twice at his watch. "That's better," he said, when his son reappeared. "Do you have the folders?"

"Why do we need the folders?"

"Just get them, all right! Good God!"

The boy went upstairs still again, and Sumrall, in the hallway, sighed heavily, already exhausted.

****

With three miles to go before they arrived for the first interview, Sumrall woke up Lewis and said they were almost there. The boy made a grunting sound, stretched his arms.

"Well, are you ready?" Sumrall said.

"No sweat."

"Promise me something, Lewis. Don't say 'no sweat' to Mr. Wall."

"Why not?"

"Because it's slang, it's commonplace. And when you address him, say 'sir.'"

Lewis had loosened his tie and was now adjusting it. "They're going to like me or they're not," he said

"You don't get accepted to these schools on your looks! And your grades aren't all that good." Sumrall took one hand off the steering wheel and rubbed his forehead. "Lewis, I want to make myself clear. By all means, be yourself. But at the same time take your candidacy seriously. Expressions like 'no sweat' can give the wrong impression, and the idea is to make a favorable impression. That's all I'm saying."

He swung the car beneath a handsome wrought-iron archway. On the left of the two brick columns supporting it, a polished brass plaque read: THE SHERWOOD SCHOOL. Founded 1839. They drove slowly along a spruce-lined drive, with expansive playing and athletic fields on one side, to a classic quadrangle surrounded by ivy-covered buildings. Huge maples, leaves red and gold, grew in the center of the quad. Sumrall pulled to the curb and parked.

"Right on time," he said, peeking under the sleeve of his jacket. He looked at his son. "Your tie's crooked."

The boy gave it a tug, centering it.

"Do you remember the headmaster's name?" Sumrall asked.

"No."

"Check the folder. If he comes in while you're talking with Mr. Wall, you'll know who it is."

"Wouldn't Mr. Wall introduce us?"

"Lewis, it can't hurt to know the headmaster's name!"

From the folder marked "Sherwood," the boy removed a pamphlet and looked through the first few pages. "Christopher W. Grosset."

"Good. Remember it," Sumrall said.

Father and son got out and walked along a flagstone path toward the largest of the ivy-clad buildings. Every few moments its heavy twin doors swung opened and students, carrying books, would come out. The boys all wore jackets and ties, with cord or khaki trousers; the girls had on skirts and sweaters. Sumrall looked the youngsters over carefully. Sherwood, he had heard, was taking only one application out of five. Feeling a heaviness of spirit, fearful his son was simply out of his league, Sumrall pulled open the right-hand door.

Immediately inside, fastened to a high, chestnut-brown door, was a sign: Admissions. A rather stout woman with rimless glasses welcomed them as they entered, asking, once introductions were finished, if Sumrall or Lewis would like something to drink. Coffee, Coca-Cola, hot chocolate? Lewis said no, Sumrall yes to coffee. The woman smiled politely and disappeared, going into an inner office, and minutes later a man came out, walking across the beige carpet and saying, "Lewis, Mr. Sumrall, welcome to Sherwood. I'm Bill Wall."

"How do you do," said Sumrall, thinking the school officer's appearance very sudden, as if he were hoping to catch the candidate—and maybe his father—in an unguarded moment.

"Lewis, nice meeting you," Mr. Wall said, and he and Lewis also shook hands.

He was young, perhaps thirty-three, with fine brown hair and splendidly blue eyes. "Beautiful day for a drive," he said.

"Glorious," said Sumrall.

"Where actually is New Falls?"

Sumrall waited, wanting to give Lewis a chance to speak up, really wanting to give him an elbow in the ribs. "Almost due west, a bit to the south—exactly eighty-three miles."

The director of admissions smiled. He was wearing a tweed jacket, charcoal-brown trousers and a red-striped tie. "Well, Lewis," he said, "let's get to know each other a little better."

"Sure."

Sumrall's eyes momentarily blurred. What kind of answer was that? It was what you said to a pal in New Falls if he asked you if you wanted to go fishing!

The woman with rimless glasses appeared with coffee, Mr. Wall escorted Lewis into his inner office, and Sumrall sat down in front of a low, mosaic table. He tasted his coffee, then picked up a faded-green Sherwood yearbook, Class of '49—one of several on the table—and flipped through the pages.

****

"I'm going to pull that one on my brother-in-law," Mr. Wall was saying twenty-five minutes later, laughing, as he and Lewis came out to the reception area.

"Maybe you know the answer," the director went on, now speaking to Sumrall who was getting to his feet. "When can a batter have four 'at bats,' go hitless, and not have it bring down his average?"

"If—if he walks?" Sumrall said.

"A walk isn't considered an 'at bat.'"

"Of course." Sumrall was frowning. "Well, ah, if—"

"On opening day, when he's batting .000 to start with. Mr. Wise Guy here—" he pointed a thumb at Lewis, "—just caught me with it, and I'm the baseball coach!"

Mr. Wall suddenly looked across the room; a sixteen-year-old girl with red hair and freckles had just walked in. "Sandy," he said, "perfect timing! Come meet the Sumralls."

At first Sumrall thought the girl's appearance coincidental, but then Mr. Wall explained that Sandy was one of Sherwood's best "tour guides" and would be happy to show Lewis around the campus. Lewis shook hands with Mr. Wall and left with the girl.

"You've got a marvelous boy there," the director of admissions said. "Outgoing, energetic, bright. You must be very proud of him."

"Well—ah, yes! Thank you."

There was a brief pause, and Sumrall thought the director of admissions was going to put out his hand and say goodbye. But he said, "Come into my office, why don't you, Mr. Sumrall. I'm sure you have some questions."

He would have preferred waiting by himself, but how could he say no? He followed the administrator into a spacious, tastefully appointed room—leather chairs and sofa, original seascapes on the rice-papered walls, a large walnut desk near the ceiling-high window.

"Sit down, Mr. Sumrall. More coffee?"

"No, thank you."

"Now, is anything on your mind?"

He felt he should say something, by way of showing interest. "If Lewis comes to Sherwood, assuming of course he gets in—"

"Let's make that assumption," said Mr. Wall with a smile.

Sumrall pressed on. "What are the steps, I mean suppose two or three schools accept a boy—or girl. Lewis has interviews scheduled at St. Crowell's and Hartwick later today. Oh, Sherwood is tops, at the top of his list—don't misunderstand me, Mr. Grosset. I'm just wondering -"

"I'm Mr. Wall."

"What did I say?"

"You said 'Mr. Grosset.' He's our headmaster."

"Of course. I'm sorry."

"It's perfectly all right."

Sumrall found himself gripping the arms of his chair. Moving his hands to his lap, he said, "What I'm trying to say—well, as to how it all started, Lewis has a second cousin once removed—I've never understood that 'removed' business but that's what Walter is—or maybe he's twice removed—" Sumrall gave a little laugh, "—anyway, Walter put the bug in Lewis's ear about going away. He's at Exeter—or is it Andover?—one or the other—and I told Lewis he could go away to a private school if he really wanted to. In all honesty, Mr. Grosset, our local high school isn't—"

He cut himself off. "Did I just say 'Mr. Grosset' again?"

"No problem."

"I'm dreadfully sorry. Anyway, we narrowed the list down to three schools. Sherwood, St. Crowell's and Hartwick. As for the others—well, take Williston. A really fine school—boys only. OK, an all-male environment is traditional among prep schools but times have changed. If a boy wants to go to school with girls, to me that's healthy. We crossed off Brink. One of the finest, but just too far away. I really enjoy watching Lewis participate in athletics, and if he went to Brink I'd have to plan visits instead of just hopping in the car." Sumrall stopped.

Mr. Wall was looking at him as if trying to figure out an abstract painting. "Your son's a golfer, he tells me."

"Yes, good too. Broke eighty this past summer consistently."

"How long has he been playing?"

"Three years now. It was just after his mother died that he picked it up. Did Lewis mention his mother?"

"No, he didn't."

"It was sudden—an accident. It was a huge loss, for both of us."

"Understandably."

Sumrall wanted to loosen his tie. "So I keep asking myself, why am I sending him away when he's all I have? It's difficult for me to answer that question. My father enrolled me at Blaydon Academy—he never even took me to *see* the god-damn school! I was lost from the start. But Lewis is different. He's the kind of kid who makes his way—"

"Yes, I believe he is," said Mr. Wall.

****

St. Crowell's was a larger school than Sherwood, looking exactly like a small, private college. Sumrall and Lewis located the admissions office, inside a stone building with great fluted columns marking its entrance, and went in. An elderly woman with small translucent teeth told them to please have a seat.

Unlike Sherwood, where Sumrall and his son were the only ones in the office, the St. Crowell's admissions office was crowded. Four other families were sitting about the room. What struck Sumrall as odd was that the women were all dressed similarly—skirts, blazers and shoes with low, layered heels. One of the men was in a blue business suit, but three others had on flannel trousers, sports jackets and loafers (one pair had tassels, another had a miniature horse-bit across the front.) Sumrall glanced at his suede, ankle-height shoes with crepe soles. A few days ago he had worn them in the rain, and now the toes were stained.

After a wait of some fifteen minutes, a tall, brittle-looking man appeared before Sumrall and his son, formally introduced himself as Mr. Wilcox, assistant to the director of admissions, and without delay invited Lewis into his office. Sumrall read magazines while waiting, his feet crossed and tucked beneath his chair.

After a somewhat shorter interview than his first, Lewis returned to the reception room with Mr. Wilcox. Whatever rigidness the assistant director had initially shown, wasn't there now. In Sumrall's opinion he seemed like a different man.

"I want you to know, Mr. Sumrall," Mr. Wilcox said, "regardless of whether Lewis comes to St. Crowell's or not, we have a golf date for next year."

"That—that's wonderful," Sumrall replied.

"He's going to give me six strokes and we're going to play fifty cent Nassaus. Right, Lewis?"

"I said three strokes."

"Sorry—so you did." Mr. Wilcox laughed. Then, glancing toward the doorway, "Oh, good. Here's Danny."

A stocky, red-haired boy came over; he would be very glad, he said, to show Lewis around the school. Lewis and Mr. Wilcox shook hands, and the youths walked off.

"Well, what a really splendid boy you have, Mr. Sumrall. So marvelously direct and open—I thoroughly enjoyed our talk."

"I'm very glad."

"Do you have any questions?"

"No. No questions. It's been a real pleasure. I—I'll just wait for Lewis."

"Please, come into my office and we can chat for a few minutes," Mr. Wilcox said.

****

At Hartwick, after delivering his son for a 3:30 appointment, Sumrall went back out and sat in the car. An hour and ten minutes later, Lewis came walking up and slid in beside him and Sumrall started the engine. Lewis said that he and Mr. McMahon had had a terrific talk. The dorm rooms and library were great but the gym wasn't nearly as modern as St. Crowell's. And the kids he'd met weren't all that friendly. Lewis didn't know why that was; they just weren't.

"Did Mr. McMahon ask for me afterward?"

"No. He didn't say anything."

"Of the three schools, which—?"

"I'm kind of tired, Dad. Can we talk later?"

"Of course."

Lewis settled back in his seat and closed his eyes, and Sumrall drove, at 6:40 parking in the detached garage to his house. He sat for a few seconds, hands idle on the wheel. Then he nudged his son. "We're home."

They walked up the path. No sooner had Sumrall unlocked the door than the telephone rang. Lewis grabbed it and Sumrall went to the liquor cabinet and took out a bottle of bourbon. Soon Lewis came into the living room, where Sumrall was sitting by one of the front window, and asked if he could go out with Jimmy.

"If you want to."

The boy ran upstairs and Sumrall didn't move in his chair, except as he lifted his glass. When Lewis came back down, he had on a navy-blue sweater and his Reeboks. "What will you be doing?" Sumrall asked.

"There's a good movie playing. Maybe afterwards we'll go for a pizza."

"Do you have any money?"

"Two dollars."

Sumrall set his drink down and took a five from his wallet. "Have a good time," he said.

"Thanks, Dad. Oh, and thanks for driving me."

"No sweat, Lewis."

The boy smiled and went to the door. At the window, Sumrall watched his son walk down their path, then turn on the street toward town.

THE FARLOW EXPRESS

When third-class Petty Officer Mulhaven left the destroyer *Villaume,* we lost an important man aboard ship, not because Mulhaven was a particular bargain (he was capable and did his job), but simply because he was the ship's barber. Now we had none at all.

Naturally the Executive Officer was worried because the *Villaume* would be leaving in less than a week for the Far East, and he didn't want to admit to the Captain that he had no one ready to take over in the barbershop. You see, Mr. Ffrench was a great man for training. He ran about three movies a week in the mess decks, on radar, first-aid, gunnery, boat handling, VD prevention, military justice, on all kinds of things, and he made each department head turn in a weekly report on what he had done on his own to further the program, the drills and exercises he'd held, the lectures he'd given. Mr. Ffrench was a thorough man. He knew every sailor aboard, how many times he'd been on report in the last quarter, what his battle station was, how

much time he had to do. The Executive Officer of the USS
Villaume had the ship's company at his finger tips.

That is, all except Mulhaven, and now he was gone.

At officers' quarters the next morning, Mr. Ffrench gave us
the word. He was a nervous, heavy man, with dull eyes the color
of old cordovan leather, and a large face that demanded a smile
to keep it from looking mean. But you seldom saw the smile,
only the small eyes and the straight thick mouth.

"I'll make it plain and simple. We need a barber." He curled
his lower lip over a cork-tipped cigarette and lit it with a silver-
cased Zippo. "I want each division officer to turn in names to
me, any likely prospects, the more on the ball they have the better. We only have a couple of days and I want that barbershop
open!"

"Why can't we just request one from the Squadron Commander?" Steve Nellis asked. He was tall, with a young, pale
face, and was Damage Control Officer on the *Villaume.* We
called him "Watertight." Watertight Nellis. He was at his best
when he could trace a leak in the ship's fire and flushing system.

"Mr. Nellis." The Exec paused. If he paused after your name
you knew you were about to get it, anywhere from thirty seconds
to five minutes. "Do you understand how this reflects on our
training program? How long did we have Mulhaven? Twenty-
seven months. It takes no genius to see we've failed somewhere!
And you want to run it all the way up to the Squadron Commander via the Captain?"

"It was a suggestion, sir," Steve Nellis said.

"I want names, not suggestions." The Exec began to breathe
quickly and you could see his meaty chest expand under his
khaki shirt. He took a deep drag on his cigarette, coughed when

he exhaled. I looked down at the dark-gray deck. We were all silent.

"All right. We see where we stand," Mr. Ffrench said. "Somewhere there's a barber right in the men we have, and we're going to find him if we have to interview every last hand aboard this ship! Are there any questions?"

There were none.

"Very well. Now get me some good names. Post!"

We saluted and went our way. My division, the second, mustered on the forward main deck when we were in port. My leading petty officer was a first-class gunner, and I heard his Irish bellow bring the men to attention as I approached. "Now square away here, sailors! Off those lifelines!" Then he turned to me and saluted. "Good morning, Mr. Baldwin."

"Good morning, Flannigan."

"All present and accounted for, sir, except Heath. Still over the hill."

"Very well."

I put the division at ease. They were a tough crew, these gunners and boatswains and torpedo men, and looking them over I didn't see any likely prospects. Still, I had to put out the word. "Listen up here. We need a ship's barber. I'm looking for anyone who thinks he could do the job."

No answer, only shuffling feet. I went on: "We're in bad straits now that Mulhaven has left, and we have to get the shop opened before shoving off Tuesday. Are there any takers?"

"Anderson wants it!" came from the outboard rank, and immediately a howl went up. "Yeah, Anderson for ship's barber!"another sailor cried out.

"Can it, you bums!" shouted Flannigan.

I looked at Anderson. He was a double hash-mark seaman, once a second class boatswain's mate who, a year earlier, had faced a court-martial for disorderly conduct ashore. Aboard ship he was an outstanding sailor. "I'll let Anderson speak for himself, like any man here," I said. After a few seconds, I turned to Flannigan. "Do you have anything for the division?"

"No, sir."

I turned back to the sailors. "Dismissed!"

****

About ten o'clock that same morning I was in my room below decks, working on an ammunition expenditure report, when I heard a light knock outside the curtain.

"Yes, come in."

One of the seamen in the Second Division entered my room, hat in hand.

"What is it, Farlow?"

"May I talk with you, Mr. Baldwin?"

"Sure, sit down."

In dungarees, Farlow pulled up the aluminum-framed chair. He was tall and thin, about twenty-one, with straw-colored hair and a sharp, New England nose. His eyes were a light blue, almost the identical color of his faded chambray shirt. I had known Farlow for over two years, ever since I'd come aboard the *Villaume,* and he had struck me then, right through till now, as a lonely young man. All his duty had been on deck. At reveille it was automatic for him to hit the brightwork, at evening "sweepers" to start a broom. And in between you could find him working, not too fast, chipping rust, laying down a coat of deck gray or washing a bulkhead. Few men outside the deck force knew him except as the skinny sailor always shining turnbuckles in the morning.

"What's on your mind?"

"Well, sir, I want you to know I'd like to strike for ship's barber."

It was the last thing I had expected him to say. "You've taken me by surprise, Farlow."

"I figured I would."

"What's behind it, just fed up with deck, generally?"

"It's more than that, sir."

He twirled his white hat in his long, loose-jointed fingers. "I would like to get off the deck force but I felt that way a year ago, even longer. This is something different. It's the first thing I've wanted, really wanted, since joining the navy."

"That's fine, Farlow, but it's not all that simple, like shifting your cleaning station from the fantail to the 0-1 level. It's a real skill being a barber; you just don't step into it."

"I know that, sir."

"And another thing, you haven't got much time left. After this cruise, you're out. Isn't that right?"

"Yes, sir."

I shook my head. "There it is, Farlow. You've spent almost three years on deck, and now at the end you want to change jobs, departments, everything all at once. I think it's too late. Cutting hair takes experience and time, and I don't honestly believe—"

"I've been practicing, Mr. Baldwin."

"Oh?"

"The boots have been sitting for me. Here, I have a list." He drew out a crumpled piece of paper from the pocket of his shirt.

I read the names, seven altogether, and recognized them as the new men straight from the Training Center in San Diego.

"I really hacked the first few, but the last two or three aren't bad," he said, pulling a little closer in the chair.

"When did you give these haircuts?"

"In the evenings, sir."

"After a full day on deck?"

"Yes, sir."

For a moment he stared at the piece of faded green carpet covering the steel deck in my room; then he looked up and spoke to me as seriously, and as sincerely, as a man could speak. "I figure I have to do this, Mr. Baldwin. The day Mulhaven left, I knew it. It came to me like that, I don't know how, laying awake in the compartment. If I let it go—" his wide, bony shoulders twisted, "—it's like giving up, Mr. Baldwin. It's like a chance you don't take because you just didn't put your hand out. I know I've only got this cruise left but that's enough—" he lowered his eyes, then raised them quickly, "—for someone to find theirself in."

All you could hear was the constant low roar of the ship's forced-air ventilators.

"I'll talk to the Exec," I said.

Mr. Ffrench was at his desk that afternoon when I went into his room. He had just stamped out a cigarette in a polished brass ashtray made from a cut-off five-inch powder case.

"Yes, Mr. Baldwin?"

"Sir, I'd like to talk to you about a barber, well, about a man who's interested."

He motioned for me to sit down, then ran his hand through his damp, graying hair. He had probably been at paper work for

110

two hours. His room was about half again as large as mine with a full-deck carpet and a stainless metal clothes locker. But it was no cooler.

"Well, finally. I don't think any one of you cares whether we get a god-damn barber or not. Do you know who Mr. Nellis gave me? *Lazzaro*. That—that animal!"

I felt the sweat rolling down my sides like little spiders.

"Well, give me the name. I haven't got all day," he said.

I took an especially deep breath. "Farlow, sir."

Mr. Ffrench looked at me for a long time. His eyes were life-less, dull, but excellent for staring. "Mr. Baldwin." Exasperation traced deep ridges across his wet brow. "If you choose to wait until five-thirty and joke with me over a couple of vodka and tonics in the O-Club, all right. But not now! Now, is there any-thing else you wish to talk about?"

"I'm not joking, Mr. Ffrench."

"Not joking! Why, Farlow can't even get a job done on deck, how in god's name do you expect him to run a barbershop? Fur-thermore—" he swung around on his swivel chair and gave me the full shot of his heavy chest—"furthermore, he's a clown. Just recall only two weeks ago, Mr. Baldwin, the incident on the star-board side, the spilling of *five gallons* of deck gray! And when he was mess-cooking for the chiefs, do you happen to remember the whole platter of steaks he sent flying when he tripped down the ladder? And what about that time—but forget it. And you want to recommend this boy for barber, you want to trust him with clippers and scissors and appointments and responsibility. I wonder about you sometimes. I really do."

"Well, Mr. Ffrench, I just thought—"

"You think too much, Mr. Baldwin!"

I got up slowly. "That may be true, sir." About to go out, I remembered the list of names Farlow had given me. "Anyway, here's a few of the men's hair he's already cut."

He took the crumpled piece of paper and looked it over. "Wonder he didn't kill any of them," he said, and turned back to his desk.

It was good to get on deck and stand in the April breeze coming in from the Pacific.

I didn't go to Farlow to tell him about my talk with the Exec. I hoped his enthusiasm would die naturally, that he'd give up the idea of becoming ship's barber and stick to being a deck hand. But two days later I noticed several of the twenty-year men in the division with a distinctive Farlow touch about their ears. Rauch, my second-class torpedo man, had severe unsymmetrical sideburns; Cobb, a boatswain third with twelve years in, couldn't say his case of "the splotches" was a mild one; and Hemsworth, a seaman who only the week before had shipped for six, was awarded for his devotion to the service by a thousand-dollar bonus and clipperscar.

Yet, even these haircuts, rough as they were, were better than having the men about deck with hair over their ears and down their necks. There would have been no "Ah's" from a visiting Admiral making a personnel inspection. On the other hand, there would be no chance he'd say to the Captain, afterwards, "Your men need haircuts." Though he'd probably ask, "Who's your barber?"

After the mess line was secured that evening, I walked into the division berthing compartment. About ten or twelve men were getting ready for the night's liberty, pulling on their tailor-mades, getting a brush-off from one of their buddies. Others, still in dungarees, sat on their deck lockers writing letters, while two shipmates strummed guitars and sang "I'm in the Jailhouse Now." And there were those already in the rack, dead to the noise and commotion, sleeping through it all as only sailors can do. They were the watch-standers, getting a few hours in before midnight.

And sure enough, Farlow was there, practicing his trade. He had set up a straight-backed chair. On one of the shiny locker tops were his tools: a pair of scissors, a black-bristled brush, an electric clipper, and a small can of talcum powder. In the chair in dungaree trousers and a bleached white T shirt sat Anderson. A bath towel covered his shoulders and was fastened in back by a large safety pin. Farlow didn't see me for several seconds. I stood there, quietly.

Finally he looked up and a big grin spread across his face. "Evening, Mr. Baldwin."

"Hello, Farlow. I see you've been busy these last few days."

"Sure have, sir."

I moved closer; the five or six deckhands standing around gave me a little room. "How you doing, Anderson?" I said. "Nervous?"

Farlow's clippers ran over the back of the sailor's neck. "I ain't no moshun pichar star, Mr. Baldwin. What do I care if he cuts me up a speck?"

Farlow snapped off the button on the electric shaver. Then he said, "I'm saving 'em all money, Mr. Baldwin. It's hard turning down a free haircut." He examined Anderson's left sideburn, took a snip at it. "And all the while the list grows. 'Course now I could really bolster it with an officer's name or two."

I felt all the men's eyes converge. I knew I needed a haircut. I was planning to get one in town tomorrow before driving out to my girlfriend's house in North Hollywood. But not one of Farlow's. My god, not one of these scalpings! She would shoot me.

"It sure is gettin' purty long, 'specially 'round the ears," said Myers, a husky blond kid from Iowa who was striking for boatswain's mate.

"Yeah, what's that they say? The officer sets the example," said a sailor known as Times Square. His first week aboard ship, he'd made it clear that his stomping ground was Forty-second Street and he knew every cop by his first name.

"Now you wouldn't wanta let us down, wouldya, sir?" Myers came back.

I scrambled for a way out. "I wouldn't but my girlfriend's waiting for me and I'm already late." I started to leave when I heard Farlow's voice above the growing clamor.

"I'm ready for you, Mr. Baldwin."

I stopped. Anderson had jumped clear and was brushing off his dungarees. "There you go, sir," he said, pointing to the chair.

"Service with a smile, Broadway style!" Times Square said, holding it for me.

I sat down. My voice seemed small as I sent up a plea to Farlow amidst the excitement in the Second Division compartment. "Just go easy on the clippers, that's all, Farlow. *Easy on the clippers.*"

By this time the entire division, as nearly as I could make out, had gathered around, and even the watch standers had given up their cherished sleep to witness the event. I heard my name, linked with Farlow's, drift like smoke up the worn ladder onto the main deck, and pictured it seeping into passageways, down scuttles, through hatches into every space on the ship: "Farlow's cutting Mr. Baldwin's hair!"

As the crowd cheers on the athlete, so the sailors on the *Villaume* cheered on Farlow. I could tell by his motions, by the way he shifted his weight and moved with deliberation—an exacting snip here, a deft whir of the clippers there—that he was experiencing a great moment. He was doing more than simply cutting my hair. For the first time since coming aboard, Farlow was doing something that was his alone.

The comments kept coming. "Now, Farlow, take it easy. He didn't put you on report last month but what you deserved it—even though you always said different."

"It'll grow back in time, that's one good thing about hair."

"Man, to think I was plannin' on hittin' the beach. This is the best show I seen in years."

"She'll wonder what injun you run into, Mr. Baldwin!"

It didn't feel as if Farlow was murdering me, although some of the remarks made me wonder. "How's it going?" I ventured at last.

"Almost done, sir."

Suddenly I felt the clippers on top of my head, not hard, not to the scalp, just skimming over the surface.

"Look at 'im go!" cried Times Square.

I panicked. "Farlow, what in god's name--"

"It's all right, sir."

I felt the clippers like tiny bugs nibbling the hair on top of my head.

"Casey Jones! Whhhooo-hoooo!" a sailor shouted.

"The Farlow Express!" announced Anderson, and there soared to the overhead the lusty voices of thirty sailors in approval.

They cheered when I went out. You might've thought I'd done something heroic. God help me, I thought, thinking of a few people I knew.

The next morning in the wardroom Steve Nellis looked me over as I sat down. "Is that a statement?"

I didn't answer. I saw the Exec's dark eyes focus on my head from the other end of the table. "Just who in hell got hold of you, Mr. Baldwin?"

"Farlow, sir."

"You are without doubt the most persistent, one-way, aggravating young officer I have ever known!"

He pointed at me with a knobby index finger. The pink color of his heavy, close-shaven face turned a light shade of purple. "Just what do you call it, that's all I want to know, Mr. Baldwin. Because you sure as hell can't call it a haircut!"

"It's a Farlow Express, sir," I said.

I spent the rest of the day confined in my stateroom. Not until four o'clock did the Exec call for me. He sat me down with a quick motion of his hand. I watched his large, fleshy jaws working before he turned to me to speak.

"I'll accept your apology, Mr. Baldwin, for your behavior at the breakfast table," he began, drawing out a cigarette and tapping it on his watch crystal.

"If I showed disrespect, I apologize, sir."

The silver-cased Zippo threw a momentary patch of light across his dark afternoon face. He inhaled deeply. "All right, but just remember we're still in port, when it's easy. After forty days at sea, and we'll be getting them, you'll find it a bit different. Even your closest friend can aggravate you when you're standing twelve hours of watch each day, and the weather's bad, and the operating's tense or dull, it doesn't make much difference. You really have to tread easy or there's going to be a lot of irritated officers and crew on the *Villaume!*"

He flicked his cigarette. "And the one it won't pay to irritate, not by any manner or means, will be me! I want you to know that now, Mr. Baldwin."

"Yes, sir," I said.

He looked at me a few seconds longer with his small, dark eyes. He had a humorless face, a kind not uncommon in the Navy when the Navy has got the better of a man. It showed the twenty-five years of sweat given to his service career, from the time he was a seaman until now, when he could wear a gold oak leaf on his collar. It was a tired face, as Mr. Ffrench was a tired man. He had served too long.

"Now about Farlow," he said, then suddenly began coughing. The cigarette made a black mark on the brass ashtray where he crushed it out.

"I have to stop," he said.

I wanted to agree with him.

"I noticed quite a few men with haircuts like yours today," he said.

"I haven't been out, sir. I don't know."

"Indians!"

I said nothing.

The Exec was staring at my hair. Then he shook his head gravely. "I only hope the boy can give a good old-fashioned trim. Because if he tries anything like that on me, he'll be one sorry sailor. Make that very clear to him. Now, to end this fiasco of a search, Mr. Baldwin, which you seem to have orchestrated, commencing tomorrow at 0800—" struggling to say the words, he fumbled with a pack of cigarettes, shook one loose, "—commencing tomorrow at 0800, Farlow is the ship's barber."

"Yes, sir," I said.

****

It rained nonstop in May and most of June, and for ten solid days on the Formosa Patrol we took water over the bow. It came in great foaming blankets and raced along the decks, shooting high into the air when it struck a scuttle or hatch, like a geyser. Then it would fall back and flow over the sides, to be caught in the sea swirling by. You watched a white-capped wave come toward you, and then saw it pass and lose itself somewhere beneath a hazy gray sky not far astern, and you heard the dull, constant whine of the wind tearing at the steel bulwarks of the bridge and felt the spray like needles in your face. You stood watches that seemed to come upon each other as fast as the waves, and you were always climbing back to the bridge to face the wind and spray and sea all over again.

At any time of day or night the *Villaume* would go to general quarters if unidentified planes or ships were closing too fast or if sonar picked up an underwater contact. The gong of the general alarm was not a disturbing noise, like an alarm clock in the morning, but a feared noise, because it yanked you with an intangible force from whatever you were doing, freezing you for a moment, and then sent you running to your battle station. And each time you went you thought this was it—the Chinese were coming across the strait to attack Formosa and there was only the *Villaume* to try and stop them.

But the *Villaume* was lucky, because the endless hours of standing watch in foul weather, or under a subtropical sun, didn't seem endless at all, as they might have, as we all thought they would. You were surprised at the absence of grumbling when the general alarm ordered the men away from their evening movie, or kept them at their battle stations for hours on end. You were amazed how the ship's work got done, the painting, the upkeep of guns and equipment, when there was hardly time to eat and catch a few hours' sleep before the P.A. system announced again and again: "Now on deck, relieve the watch!"

And then you began to see why, and then finally you knew. The USS *Villaume* had Farlow.

Secure and dry on the second deck, his barbershop became the meeting place on board ship, where the men gathered, ten or twelve at a time, to smoke a cigarette or drink a Coke, and to talk. Farlow had painted the bulkheads a high-toned white, which he kept as clean as shiny porcelain, and the deck was a deep green. The stanchions at the foot of the ladder were like peppermint sticks, and against two of the bulkheads benches were set up, each of which seated five men. The barber's stool with a red leather top was in the after part of the space, and secured to the bulkhead at chest height was the cabinet. Of everything in the shop (including the large photo of Marilyn Monroe) Farlow was proudest of his cabinet.

He had taken a discarded aluminum locker from one of the sleeping compartments and given it the triple treatment of steel wool, elbow grease, and metal polish. It was about two feet high and a foot deep and inside were three gleaming trays on which his tools lay like a doctor's instruments. Two new clippers with three different heads you could put on or take off, three scissors, two wooden-handled brushes, several differently shaped combs, a enamel wisp with genuine bristles, and a large-sized can of Prince Matchabelli scented powder.

He was in his shop seven hours every day, except Sundays, to give his haircuts, but even after he was through working the shop stayed open, although then it wasn't a shop, but a club. To be a member made you feel something you would not wish to lose, when you were thousands of miles from home. And to be a member all you had to do was get a Farlow Express.

By the first of June there were two hundred members, all with the haircuts distinctively leveled on top. Never before had the crew been so close. On the cruise to the Med the previous winter, there had been continual grumbling about bad weather, "navy" chow, and constant talk about getting back to civilian life. And the Med cruise was a pleasure trip compared to the one we were now on. Fresh water, made by the ship from sea water, was scarce. You were allowed a three-minute shower but hardly enough water trickled down from showerheads to get wet. It wasn't an easy tour of duty, but as long as men could visit Farlow once, sometimes twice a week, they took destroyer life in the Far East pretty much in stride. I ducked in and out of his shop as much as anyone.

"Next," Farlow said, shaking out the barber's cloth.

Second-class quartermaster Stanzione took his place on the stool. "Make it a little shorter on top, Farlow, like you done Bronko's."

"The sun's awful strong there on the bridge, you're sure?" Farlow said.

"You need brains to get a stroke," the boilerman next in line piped up.

"Lacking any yourself," Stanzione said as Farlow started in, "how would you know?"

"I seen you in the Blue Orchid in Sasebo."

"So?"

"That little Suzysan had you wrapped around her little finger."

"She sure did. It was great."

"Like they say, there's a sucker born every minute," the boilerman said.

"Eat your heart out, Trippico," the quartermaster came back.

The barbershop was alive with banter, joking, laughs—men talking cars and baseball, arguing the case for Japanese over American women, celebrating the three-quarter mark of the cruise. Farlow snapped on the third head to the clippers, giving Stanzione the final touch; that was when everybody started hollering at once, "Whhhooo-hoooo!"

In the wardroom, Nellis was second after me to get the Farlow Express, followed by the Duke and Chapel Hill duo, Ensigns Goldman and Cummings. Then it really caught on. No one expected the Commanding Officer to get a Farlow Express. He liked to see his crew happy but he had other things on his mind and was a loner anyway. As for Mr. Ffrench, he was just plain stubborn, an angry old mustang, and we had to live with him, hawser by winch, every day. He got his trim once a week religiously, but never in the barbershop. Over the loudspeaker you would hear: "Now Farlow, lay to the Executive Officer's stateroom."

In the wardroom it always got quiet whenever he came in for a cup of coffee. He would sit down at the felt-covered table and light a cigarette, and whoever was there at the time—well, we would look around at each other, guessing who it was going to be; whose turn to take the exec's frustration. Goldman, Baldwin, Cummings, Hardenburg, Nellis--

"*Mr. Nellis.*"

"Sir."

"Have you got the problem made up for the Damage Control Quarterly Exercise, in accordance with CINCPACFLEET's latest instruction?"

"I'm working on it, sir."

"I want to see it tomorrow by ten hundred!"

"Yes, sir."

The months steamed slowly by. The supply of books became exhausted and movies started to come back to us for the third time, having gone around and around in the fleet. Mr. Ffrench loved movies. He never missed one, no matter how bad. But even the Exec, who could easily sit through a class C twice, began complaining, and then one sweltering night in August he hit the overhead.

Actually, it had all been building up inside him for weeks, the hot slow zig-zag steaming on the Formosa Patrol, the strict water hours, the lack of mail for nineteen days, the worn out movies. We felt it too, but we felt it together. There was no one with Mr. Ffrench. He was alone on the ship, apart from the officers, at odds with the crew. He barked continually, at some poor seaman who didn't have his white hat on walking about the deck or at any of his junior officers whose best, no matter what we were doing, just wasn't good enough.

When "Ma and Pa Kettle on Vacation" appeared on the screen Mr. Ffrench jumped up, his khaki shirt dark-stained with sweat and his heavy body shaking. "Not again! Turn that pro-jector off!" He singled out Ensign Goldman, the movie officer.

"It's some god-damn nerve you have showing this picture three times in one month, let me tell you, Mr. Goldman! This is one of the few pleasures we have on ship and you go botch it up by your careless selection! I've seen incompetent individuals in my day, but never—"

Suddenly he stopped, as if at that moment he became aware of himself, like a person about to be photographed. Sweat lay heavy on his gray hairline and through his fleshy knuckles you could see white as he held on the back of his chair. The seconds that followed, lengthened immeasurably by the silence, de-manded we look elsewhere than at the miserable, soaked hulk of the Executive Officer of the USS *Villaume*. Then, just as quickly as he had exploded, he left the wardroom.

The next morning Mr. Ffrench didn't show up for breakfast, but an hour later, when I was on the bridge standing the forenoon watch, this word was passed over the P.A. system: "Now Farlow, lay to the Executive Officer's stateroom."

A cool drizzle was falling like silvery spider webs from the sky. "'Now just a trim, Farlow,'" Ensign Cummings, the junior officer of the deck, said to me. "Can't you hear him?"

"I can hear him."

I didn't feel like talking anymore, so I walked over to the port side of the bridge and rested against the bulwark. I watched the sea, smooth as a clouded mirror, break into a thousand flashing pieces before the bow of the *Villaume*. It was so calm and quiet, you could feel the vibrations of the steam turbines deep within the ship. Through the overcast sky the sun filtered weakly, and the halyards tugged on the yardarms weakly too, because the breeze that fanned us on the bridge was caused only by the slow forward motion of the ship.

I became aware of an officer standing beside me, a large man, leaning with his elbows on the forward bulwark, peering into the misty air. I turned, and for a moment didn't recognize him, even though his face and size and coloring were Mr. Ffrench's. It was his hair that was so different. Cut short all around and made flat on the top.

"Good morning, Mr. Baldwin," he said.

For a moment I found it difficult to speak. "Good morning, sir."

"How's our ETA coming?"

"Still holding at fifteen hundred to Buckner Bay."

"You'll like Okinawa. Quiet, really pleasant. It'll give us a couple of good days' rest."

"I'm glad to know that, sir."

He stepped into the pilot house, studied the chart on the quartermaster's table, decided everything was in order and left the bridge. I stayed on the port wing, picturing a tall skinny kid in dungarees and chambray shirt twirling his white hat in his hands.

****

On a cool November morning we arrived back in Long Beach, twelve days over half a year from the day we'd left. They had a band playing for us and some of the tugs in the harbor were spouting water. The piers were jammed with people, and when we put down the brow they came aboard. It was almost frightening seeing so many red fingernails holding on the rail pushing toward us.

My girlfriend was there. I didn't see her until she was right next to me, because the quarterdeck was so crowded. I had forgotten how pretty she was.

A great many of the men were due to get out, and Farlow was one of them. I had the OOD in-port watch three mornings later when he came up and laid his white canvas seabag on the deck.

"So long, Mr. Baldwin" he said.

"Best of luck to you, Farlow."

"If you ever get to Alstead, I'll give you the best shave and haircut in New Hampshire."

"I might just show up."

"And for you, Mr. Baldwin, on the house." He smiled that dry grin that encompassed his face and ended up shining in his light-blue eyes. In one motion he swung his seabag onto his left shoulder. Then he looked at me and said, "Thank you, Mr. Baldwin."

He saluted and I returned the salute, and as he walked off the quarterdeck of the *Villaume* he stopped midway on the brow and saluted the National Ensign flying from the fantail. When he reached the pier he turned and waved.

"So long, Farlow!" cried Anderson, who was the Boatswain's Mate of the Watch.

IT CAN BE DID

When I landed a job in 1974 as an assistant professor of English at New Falls State, Kate and I sold our house in Wichita and bought a fixer-upper in New Falls, N.Y. Clearly we needed help. I called a local carpenter named Oliver Moore and he came by the house in an old panel truck a couple of days later. I went out to the driveway to meet him. Before he got out, I saw him lift a small paper bag to his mouth. What was I going to do, fire him on the spot? He was a wiry black man, in jeans and a rough shirt, a long-billed fishing cap on his head. I was skeptical. To see if I liked his work, I told him that I wanted louvers installed in the high peaks of the house. No easy job as I saw it. Oliver looked up at the gabled roof, studied the job for a moment, and said, "It can be did."

He worked all day. I was impressed with his work, liked what he charged, and immediately began mentioning other jobs my wife and I wanted done.

We began seeing a lot of Oliver's truck in our driveway. He put a new roof on the house, built a back porch, finished our basement, sanded floors, installed new cabinets and counters in the kitchen, made built-in bookshelves for the living room and my study, and painted the house inside and out. Kate and I thought the world of Oliver.

Sometimes after a day's work he and I would sit on the porch, have a beer, talk fishing, gardening. I considered him a friend. My daughter, a senior at New Falls High, thought I patronized Oliver and told me, in no uncertain words, that I was a "closet snob," the college professor in his refurbished Civil War house having a beer with a black man who lived in an ungainly doublewide on the other side of town. The only reason I befriended Oliver, Lisa said, was because he charged me peanuts! I told her she was wrong, told her vehemently she was wrong, and wondered, afterward, why I responded to her accusation so pointedly.

Oliver continued working for us—a house is never finished. Then, sitting on the porch one afternoon, maybe ten years after my family and I had moved to New Falls, I heard the crunching of driveway stones—Kate, home early from her job. It was the Friday at the start of the Memorial Day weekend. I turned to greet her. To my surprise, it wasn't my wife coming up the porch steps; it was Oliver, dressed, not in work clothes, as from a job, but in clean gray trousers and a snappy green shirt.

"Saw your car," he said, "thought I'd stop by."

"Glad you did. Grab a chair. Can I get you anything?" It was a warm, muggy day. I was having a glass of tonic water with lime and lots of ice.

"No, thanks."

"What's up?"

"My grandson is coming up from Georgia."

"Wonderful. How old is he now?"

"Ten. I'm taking him fishing."

"Of course you are. Great."

"I had an accident with my boat," Oliver said. "Taking it off my truck the other day, it got away from me and landed on a rock. Hove the side right in."

"That's too bad. Can you repair it?"

"It's too beat up," he said. "Sears was having a sale and I bought a new one."

"That's taking the bull by the horns."

"I'm on my way to the capital," he said.

I frowned. "Why in hell would you be doing that, Oliver? Of all days."

"I need numbers for the boat."

"Go to a hardware store."

"First you have to know what numbers to get."

"How do you find out?"

"By registering the boat," he said. "The numbers they give you are the numbers you put on it."

"Can't you register it locally?"

"You mail the form or go in person," Oliver said. "What with work and buying the boat and problems at home, I forgot to do it."

Albany was sixty-five miles away. I glanced at my watch. "Well, you have a little time, Oliver," I said, "not a hell of a lot."

"Going to the capital by myself, I'm not sure it can be did," he said.

I had only heard him use the comment, at the start of every new job, in a positive, upbeat way. "Then don't go."

"I have to take the boy fishing."

"Can't you fish from the shore?"

"I could. It's not the same thing."

It began to register. "Are you asking me to go with you, Oliver?"

"If it's not asking too much."

He could sign his name, a squiggle on the back of a check. I'd seen it many time. Could he read, could he write? He had grown up in south Georgia, had taken his first job as a roofer's helper at eleven. How much schooling he'd actually had, I didn't know. As I mulled it over, I began thinking that Oliver, for any number of reasons, saw the state capital as a scary place. He was leaning on me.

I heard myself saying, "Sorry, I'm not up to it, Oliver." What I said was, "Let me write my wife a note."

****

He drove an old Dodge pickup with a cap over the payload. In it were boxes of nails, asphalt shingles, a couple of saw horses, a step ladder and all manner of hand tools. The bench seat in the cab was patched with duct tape and the radio was hanging loose, dangling on wires from the dashboard. The ash-tray lay heavy in butts. I searched for a seatbelt but Oliver told me the truck didn't have any and lighted an unfiltered Camel.

We moved along at about forty on the Thruway, an endless stream of cars and campers, and sometimes, for no apparent reason, we had to slow to ten mph. We weren't making good time. By simple math, I had us arriving in the capital at 3:45, but that wasn't going to happen. We talked about fishing, about tools and construction, and Oliver mentioned that one day twenty-five years ago a nail had snapped as he was pulling it and had shot up hitting him in the right eye; he was 80% blind in it. I had always wondered why he squinted so when taking measurements. It wasn't something you told somebody when you showed up for a carpentry job. Oliver said he'd played pro baseball on an all-black team in Stanton, Georgia. Centerfield. Ten dollars a game. Had hopes of making it to the Negro League. He was fast, stole bases, good bunter; but then the accident with his eye and that was it. We were nearing the capital and took exit 24 but, on the ramp, were held up by an accident. Finally we got going again, and it was then I realized that Oliver didn't know where he was going. I suggested he pull over. I asked the first person walking by on the city streets, a heavy-set man in a pocket T, if he knew where the offices were for registering boats.

"I can't say for sure about boats. But for motor vehicles you want the State Office Building."

"How do you get there?"

"Hook your first left. Go three traffic lights, turn right. That'll put you on Cathedral. Just remember if you hit the Sears plaza you've gone too far."

Oliver took his first left and, glancing at my watch, I told him to push it a little. Ahead of us, the sky was starting to darken. We made it to Cathedral, crowded with vehicles of every type and size, and at one intersection Oliver braked for an amber and I told him to keep going. When we pulled into the big parking lot before the State Office Building, it was 4:20. We hurried to the entrance and pushed open the glass doors; in the distance came the rumble of thunder.

The massive lobby was a panorama of fluorescent lights and marble. People were milling about, waiting in lines, filling out forms. At the information desk in the center of the floor, Oliver told a gray-haired woman that he wanted to register a boat. She pointed to a sign at the extreme end of the lobby: New Registrations, Non-Automobile. We walked rapidly across the floor. There was a small line at the non-automobile window, and Oliver waited until his turn came. I was starting to relax. He would have his "numbers" and I was happy for him. As he slid his forms over the counter, the clerk stole a glance at the big clock on the wall. He was a young man, not yet 30, with pudgy cheeks and shiny dark hair. He flipped through Oliver's papers, as if looking for a certain document. I was standing just to one side. The clerk raised his brown, humorless eyes and said to Oliver: "Where's the sales receipt?"

"The what?"

"The sales slip for your boat."

"Ain't it there?"

"If it was here, would I be asking you for it?"

Oliver was silent. The clerk gave him a second, then looked over Oliver's shoulder. "Next."

"Excuse me," I said. "I'm with Mr. Moore and we've just driven seventy miles to get here—"

"I can't help you, sir," the clerk said, cutting me off. "I need the sales receipt. Next."

I didn't step aside. "Do you think Mr. Moore stole the boat?"

"How he got the boat is his business. I need the sales receipt."

"Why?"

"As proof he paid the tax."

"Would they have sold him the boat if he hadn't paid the tax?"

"I need proof."

I looked at Oliver. "What did the boat cost?"

"$629.99."

"Times seven and a half percent," I said to the clerk. "That's roughly—forty-seven dollars. Figure it out exactly, and Mr. Moore will pay you."

"Sorry. *Next!*"

A woman in a pair of lemon stretch slacks squeezed past me and Oliver. I could see the disappointment etched on his face. "It's my own fault, I should of known," he said.

I saw myself saying "too bad" and going with him out to his truck. But something kicked in, kept me from saying it. Oliver had put faith in me, and I didn't want to let him down. His grandson was arriving. Spotting pay telephones across the lobby, I said, "Come on."

We ran over. From the local directory I found the number for the local Sears, dropped in a quarter, dialed and asked for "boats" when the store answered. Oliver and I waited. Finally a man was saying: "Sporting goods."

"I'm calling from the State Office Building on Cathedral Avenue" I said. "I'm trying to register a boat I bought at Sears— a different Sears—only I left the sales receipt at home. Can you help me?"

"In what way?"

"Can you issue me a duplicate receipt?"

"I'd need the information," the clerk said.

"What information?"

The man sighed; there were obviously customers about and he wasn't going to make any commissions on the phone. "The date of purchase," he said. "Then the name and model number of the boat, the price you paid, the sales tax, and finally the ring number."

"What's the ring number?"

"The number of the original receipt. I'm very busy right now—"

"Just tell me your name."

"Walter."

"Thank you," I said. Hanging up, I asked Oliver if someone at his house could find the sales slip.

"I don't rightly know where I put it."

"What Sears did you buy the boat from?"

"The one in Lynwood."

"Do you have any change? I need coins."

He had a pocketful. I glanced at the clock. 4:29. Just then a clap of thunder seemed to shake the whole building. Through the front windows night had suddenly fallen. I got the number for the Lynwood store from information. Oliver handed me quarters and dimes. "Sporting Goods," I said.

"That line is busy."

"This is an emergency!"

"Sir, the line is busy."

I took a deep breath. "Please keep trying."

Outside, lightning crashed, followed immediately by thunder. Scores of people were standing at the windows, looking out. Finally a woman picked up and I launched my request. "A week or so ago I bought a boat in your department. I'm in Albany right now, trying to register it but I forgot my sales slip. My name is Oliver Moore."

"Oh, yes, Mr. Moore," the woman said. "You bought the 13-foot Kingfisher."

I glanced at Oliver. "I did. Can you locate the sales slip?"

"I believe so."

"Wonderful," I told her. "Once you have it, phone the Sears on Cathedral Boulevard here in Albany. Ask for Walter in Sporting Goods. Give him the information on the sales receipt, including the *ring number*, and he'll make out a duplicate."

"The store is very crowded. Maybe later—"

"I understand, but you have to do it now," I said. "We'll go to the Albany Sears, pick up the receipt. Then we have to shoot back to the State Office Building, all by five."

"I'll see what I can do," she said.

"May I have your name?"

"Brenda."

"Thank you, Brenda," I said. Then, to Oliver, "Let's go."

We ran through the office building out into the storm. The rain was coming down in sheets—thunder, great flashes of lightning. He started up the engine. My kingdom for a seatbelt! Oliver moved out of the parking lot. Before we merged with Cathedral, he told me there was a bottle in the glove compartment. Would I unscrew the cap? He needed a nip. I didn't argue with him. He lifted the pint to his lips. Some nip. "Go ahead, take one," he said.

I felt like one but put the bottle away. Then we were on Cathedral, heading north. A large metal sign, advertising Goodyear Tires, rattled across the thoroughfare. Cars were stalled and a good number had pulled over to the shoulder. Oliver plowed through a long pool of water—running a traffic light while at it. He reached out his hand and I passed him the bottle and he had a second hit. The sound of a horn blaring behind us was deafening. We came so close to a collision that the word "Freightliner," on the monstrous hood of the semi, looked like a silver crown on

Oliver's head. I tucked the gin away and, when I looked up, saw the Sears Plaza.

"Oliver, get over! We're here!"

He swerved, another near miss. Blaring of horns. In the parking area, he cut around a downed tree and I told him to pull up to the main entrance and park in front of the No Parking sign. We got out and ran inside where we found ourselves surrounded by refrigerators and kitchen ranges. I saw a salesman who, when he saw us, looked the other way. We ran through TV & Radio, Men's, Teen Fashions, Shoes & Boots, Women's, Furniture, and finally there it was—Sporting Goods! A chunky, thick-necked man was discussing canoe paddles with a rangy chap with hollow cheeks. It wasn't polite to break right in, but I broke in.

"Excuse me, are you Walter?"

"I'll be right with you," he said.

"Look, I'm Oliver Moore. I need the sales slip Brenda from the Lynwood Sears just called you about."

"Just let me finish with this gentleman."

"There isn't time," I said.

"Hey, Mac, buzz off," said the man with hollow cheeks.

"Walter, all I need is the sales slip for my boat. Did Brenda call you?"

"Hey, buddy," the customer came back, "*buzz the fuck off!*"

The way he was holding the paddle, at that moment, bore more resemblance to lacrosse than canoeing. "Sir, you're a sportsman, right?" I said. "Would you want to deny a fellow sportsman the joy of fishing with his grandson over the weekend?"

He had no immediate answer. Then Walter was saying, "Here you go, Mr. Moore."

For all I know the slip was all X's and O's. "Thanks," I said, and we were gone. Back on Cathedral, everywhere you looked, lights were swirling, flashing. Oliver almost rammed a trooper's vehicle stopped at an accident, and his gear in the payload area slammed forward. He reached out his hand and I passed him the bottle. Whatever happened to Prof. Jeff Forrester, people in New Falls would ask. A private, conservative man, an expert on Transcendentalism in 19th Century America, driving recklessly with an intoxicated journeyman, Oliver Moore, in the state capital in the midst of a dangerous storm. Whatever it was, may they both rest in peace. In a note to his wife he had said, "K, went to Albany with Oliver. Too crazy to explain. J."

On a prayer, and a little gin, we made it back to the State Office Building. Oliver, now fully in the game, pulled up to the main entrance. A uniformed guard was crossing the marble floor inside, ready to lock up for the day. We beat him by three steps, kind of ducking around him in an end sweep. He was a stolid man and took note, looking at us dubiously. The big clock on the far wall read 4:57.

I handed Oliver the sales slip and we ran the length of the lobby. The clerk with the fat cheeks and slick dark hair was just leaving his window. Oliver ran up, waving the receipt. "I got it!" he sang out.

The clerk glanced at the clock, grumbled, and looked at two smiling individuals. We were the nicest people he'd dealt with all day. He gave the slip a quick once-over, initialed it, then did something neither of us understood. He slid the slip across the counter, turned from his window and started walking away.

"What about my numbers?" Oliver cried out.

"I only verify the tax," the clerk said. He pointed. "Over there."

We spun around. Across the lobby were ten grilled windows, as at a bank; in each, now, was an opaque panel. Half the fluorescent lights in the great room suddenly went out. On automatic pilot, I ran across the marble floor and clambered up onto the counter, stood there looking over the barricaded windows hoping to see someone in the office area; but all of the 20-odd desks were empty. The Memorial Day holiday had started for state employees.

"Hey, you!" yelled the stolid guard starting across the floor. "Get down!"

Just then a young woman with long brown hair, in a yellow dress, entered the office through a remote doorway, walked over to one of the desks and opened a drawer. "Miss!" I shouted, and she looked up, startled.

"I know it's after five but we've tried—it isn't like we just got here," I said. "We've been through hell and back trying to get it done and now we have everything in order and my friend Oliver Moore wants to take his grandson fishing over the weekend in his new boat and all he needs is the registration—"

The guard was tugging viciously at my trouser leg. "Get down from there!"

"Miss, please. Not for me—do it for Oliver." I waved him over—

I was dragged to the floor and ushered the full length of the lobby. At the main door, the guard told me to consider myself lucky he hadn't called the police, then tossed me out. The storm was ending; it was still raining but letting up. Oliver was inside, alone. I peered through the big window. He was at the counter, talking. Anything could still go wrong. Whoever you are, I thought, young woman in yellow with brown hair, give Oliver his numbers.

The transaction seemed to be over and he moved away. He didn't walk, he didn't run, he danced across that great marble floor, waving the card. I had my hand raised in a kind of power salute and the guard was shaking his head skeptically. He opened the door, and Oliver came out and we gave each other bear hugs.

"I never thought it could be did," he said.

"I wasn't sure it could be did," I came back.

We stood there laughing. At his truck I said, "Oliver, give me the keys."

He passed them over. In the passenger's seat he took out his pint, raised it toward me as I started the engine, and had a nip. He was talking away, happy. Oh, he was happy! He helped himself to another hit when we reached the Thruway and pretty soon after that he fell asleep. The alignment of his pickup kept tugging at my arms, but I stayed in lane and chauffeured Oliver safely home.

THE CLIFF WALK

A yellow and black minibus is waiting for us at the Monterey airport, and with two other couples Penny and I get on for the final leg of our journey to the Esalen Institute in Big Sur. Penny's a journalist and is under contract to write a story on the institute for *Psychology Today*. Her editor at the magazine gave her an OK to bring along her husband, who could take a workshop of his choice. The idea of "participating" at Esalen wasn't important to me but to be a sport I leafed through their catalog and chose "Tapping the Inner Self."

I'm a small-town lawyer who hasn't had a vacation in years and the idea of getting away with my wife to a scenic corner of America, all expenses paid? Here we are: rolling along the California coast, skirting great cliffs and passing long stretches of rock-dotted beaches...and a glittering Pacific Ocean.

It isn't long before our driver pulls off the highway, follows a winding driveway and comes to a stop in front of a sprawling glass-and-cedar building. We're the second couple in line, and a cheery young woman with freckled cheeks enters our names—

ANTHONY ROBINSON

Mr. and Mrs. Donald Williams of Woodbridge, New York. She wishes us a pleasant stay and gives us a key and directions to our room, 17 Garden View.

We pick up our bags, follow a narrow path and come to a string of motel-like units. A park bench is just outside our door; directly across from it, on a lower level, is a large area of cultivated land that I take as a vegetable garden. Our room isn't much—a couple of chairs and bureaus, a small desk and wall-to-wall indoor/outdoor carpeting. A large plate window looks out at the garden and manages to catch a sliver of the Pacific.

After we unpack and freshen up, Penny decides to test the bed, sitting on it and giving it a bounce, or as much of one as she can—she tips the scales at 105. She has short dark-brown hair that has a natural curl to it and periwinkle-blue eyes. We've been married for two years, the second time for each of us. Her first husband was an executive in a freight-shipping enterprise, loved "the ponies," was closer to his bookie than his wife. Fired from his job, he got drunk in an Albany bar and died in a car crash driving home. As for my first go at marriage, my wife, a therapist, jilted me for a therapist she met at a conference in Buffalo. They hadn't merely clicked; the chemistry between them "moved heaven and earth"—Gail's words as she told me about Albert Bleier. I took an apartment, intending to file for divorce; their relationship blew up after four months. He'd deceived her—he wasn't a divorced man, he was a married man with a family. What hurt most, what cut Gail deepest, was the shattering of the dream she shared (thought she shared) with Bleier: they would travel to centers and institutes around the world as a team of therapists. From everything, she had nothing. That was how it hit her. Thinking of our children and loving Gail, I would

142

have gone back with her—but for the fact that she took an emotional nosedive in the weeks after the blowup, didn't pull out of it, and committed suicide.

Penny stops bouncing on the bed. "Firm, but not too."

"Just the way I like it."

"Don, let's try the hot springs. Esalen is famous for them."

"Sure."

Her periwinkles are shining. "I didn't mean right away," she says.

****

The freckle-faced young woman in the office gives us directions: Go through the dining hall, turn left on the terrace, and cross a small Oriental bridge. The springs are a third of the way down a sloping shell path. Staying on it to the end would take you to the beach, she says.

The dining room has twenty tables, each with settings for ten. On the terrace people are sitting and standing around, enjoying the late-afternoon sunshine and a spectacular view of the Pacific. We cross the Oriental bridge and pick up the footpath. On our left stand a half-dozen cedar-sided buildings with large windows; clearly it's where workshops take place. To the right people are sitting on the rocks and boulders of a great cliff. A man in red shorts is doing a free-spirited dance, jumping from one rock to the next. Far out (and far below) surfers are catching big California waves.

At the springs we enter a large cave; it's steamy and dim and we're told by an attendant to hang clothes on a convenient hook, shower, then use any of the half-dozen tubs available to us. Finished with our shower, we choose a tub that isn't too crowded and, trying not to appear self-conscious, Penny and I step in and sit down next to each other. The water is hot, almost uncomfortably so at first. Three other women and two men are already soaking.

Greetings and first names are exchanged. Then come questions. For how long are we staying? A week, Penny says. Whose groups are we in? Penny says she's with Geoffrey Greene in "The Soma, Key to Psychic Awareness."

"I'm with Greene also," a woman with chubby white shoulders says in a Southern drawl.

"Then we'll be seeing each other," Penny says.

"How about you?" a woman, whose hair resembles a grape leaf, asks me.

"Tapping the Inner Self."

"Leonard Brontsky! Fabulous!" the woman comes back. "He is so incredibly in touch with the universal life force."

"Really?"

"Oh, yes. Definitely."

"Where y'all from?" the woman with chubby shoulders inquires.

"Woodbridge. It's near Albany," Penny says.

"Albany, *Georgia*?" Her eyes brighten.

"Sorry to disappoint," my wife says with a smile. "New York."

****

For breakfast our first morning I have home-grown strawberries with fresh cream, two eggs over easy and four strips of Canadian bacon, and Penny has whole-grain cereal topped with raisins and a side of blueberry yogurt. At ten minutes to nine we leave the hall and cross the Oriental Bridge. At Building B we stop; it's where she is meeting Geoffrey Green. "Well, see you," she says. She has her camera and a spiral notebook.

"Here goes nothing," I say.

"Relax, see what happens," Penny says. "I love you, Don."

I take another fifty steps and enter Building C, finding Room 5. Big windows open to the cliff and, beyond it, the ocean. The floor is covered with pumpkin-colored, wall-to-wall carpeting. Some fifteen people are sitting on it using large cushions, scattered everywhere, as rests or props. I find an open place in the circle, sit there, my eyes lowered. People are talking quietly among themselves; then suddenly the room goes quiet. A man about forty-five with rich dark hair and a neat black beard, brimming with health and self-assurance, strides in. He stands, while we sit.

"I have to report, with alarm and sadness," the man says, "that Leonard Brontsky was in an automobile accident yesterday afternoon. I understand that he's in the hospital in stable condition."

A groaning, a shaking of heads in disappointment. The man continues: "The Esalen Institute's office has instructed me to report that anyone wanting their money back only has to ask. Personally, I hope you'll stay in the group. I'm a practicing psychotherapist, a psychologist with many years' experience. I've just come from a two-week engagement at the Redwood Mental Health Center south of San Francisco where I conducted a workshop for professional therapists, and Esalen called me last night to ask if I were free to stand in for Dr. Brontsky. I said I'd be honored but I wouldn't be able to fill his shoes."

People in the circle smile; some laugh. The new therapist is winning people over; clearly he's skilled at it. I have never prided myself on "reading" people—Gail was uncanny at it—but he strikes me as too skilled, too into himself. The women in the circle aren't thinking so; they seem delighted.

"Let me introduce myself," the man says, sitting down in the circle, crossing his legs comfortably. "I'm Albert Bleier."

It's as if I'm on a narrow bridge that's swaying in the wind. I reach for a railing. What I come up with is a maroon cushion. A voice tells me to sit tight.

"I want to start our workshop by going around the circle," Bleier says. "Tell us your name, first name is fine. Maybe you'd like to say what brings you to Big Sur. I'll start with you," he says, gesturing to a baldheaded man with a trim gray mustache.

"My name is Barney," the man says. "I'm here from Tucson. I'm interested in understanding myself better—certain aspects of my nature bother me, especially how I deal with intimacy."

"Thank you, Barney."

The next person speaks, then the next. Then it's my turn: "I'm Don."

"What brings you to the Esalen Institute, Don?"

"I'm not sure."

"But you're here."

"I am."

"Can you give us a clue as to why?"

"Destiny."

People laugh. Bleier laughs and continues around the circle. After everyone has spoken, he talks about what he wants to achieve during the week, his goals—making each of us more knowledgeable of ourselves, more attuned to our strengths and weaknesses, when we leave Esalen. "Besides meeting here on a daily basis," he goes on, "we'll put in a couple of hours in the

Esalen vegetable garden Thursday afternoon—fabulous natural therapy. On Friday we'll be doing the exercise Leonard Brontsky originated several years ago, the renowned Cliff Walk. Right now I want to start working with you on an individual basis."

A woman about 45 with short sandy hair and a small, determined set to her chin, rises from the circle and goes to the center of the room, sits down and faces Bleier, says she's Eileen, divorced twice and currently separated from her third husband. She's disillusioned in relationships, in men generally. Life isn't holding any glow for her, any promise.

"Say this, Eileen," Bleier says. "'I feel that all men are jerks.'"

"I feel all men are jerks!"

"Say this, 'I have no respect for men.'"

She repeats the line. Evidently it's his method of working. It continues: Bleier telling her what to say, Eileen saying it. Then he says. "Say this: 'All men are creeps, in my opinion, because I don't feel good about myself.'"

She says the line.

"How does saying that feel to you?" Bleier asks.

"It hurts."

"'I can't love anyone unless I love myself.' Say that, Eileen."

She says it and breaks into tears, and Bleier comforts the dear woman in his arms.

At 12:30 Bleier says the workshop has got off to an excellent start and he'll see us at 2:00. Everyone leaves the room; other groups are also breaking for lunch and people are heading for the terrace, chit-chatting away. I'm walking along but not talking to anyone (except myself). Seeing me, as I step onto the terrace,

Penny comes right over. "How was it, how did it go?" she asks, eagerly.

"Brontsky was in an automobile accident. Nothing too serious but he won't be doing the workshop."

"Bummer! I was hoping to catch him for an interview," Penny says. "Who's the substitute?"

I spot him at the far end of the terrace talking with a woman in violet who keeps nudging her blond hair off her face. "Albert Bleier," I say.

"What? You're kidding."

"I'm not. He's here at Esalen."

"How troubling for you, Don!"

"I know."

When Penny and I started going together and into the first year of our marriage, the topic of Gail and her affair with Bleier would come up on occasion, and never ended well. The only fights we ever have are over my first wife. Something still isn't settled.

"What are you going to do, Don?"

"I haven't decided."

"You can always shift to a different workshop," Penny says.

"That's a possibility." Shifting topics, "How was Green?"

"Brilliant. I see him as the lead to my story." Then she says, "Don, I have to say something."

"OK."

"Try to remember that I'm here professionally. If my husband were to punch Bleier in the nose—"

"Don't worry about it."

"Let's have lunch," Penny says.

****

In the afternoon session, a woman about forty with orange hair and an abrasive voice tells Bleier she's tired of being bossy and opinionated. She wants to change, to become a softer person, but doesn't know how. "Say this line, Judy," Bleier says. "'I like being a bitch.'"

"I like being a bitch."

"'Because it protects me. Bitches don't get hurt.'"

"It protects me. Bitches don't get hurt."

"'Underneath I'm a sensitive, vulnerable human being.' Say that, Judy."

"Underneath I'm a sensitive, vulnerable human being."

"Excellent. How does that feel?"

"For the first time I see myself so clearly."

Bleier waits for a new person to speak up; it's Barney. They talk about intimacy. Intimacy means letting down your guard, Bleier says. "Barney, say this."

When the afternoon session ends I hurry out for a breath of sea air, following the long, down-sloping path past the hot baths to the beach. The tide is out and I walk by massive boulders at the base of the cliff, finally coming to a sandy cove directly beneath the institute that seems to invite me in. I sit, stare out at a frothy Pacific—thinking back. When Gail wouldn't stop seeing Bleier, I moved out and took an apartment. During that time, I began "visiting" my daughters in Woodbridge—sometimes taking them to dinner and the movies, sometimes to my place for the night. At the start of one such visit, as the girls were piling into my car, a metallic-gray Porsche pulled up and parked in front of the house and Bleier stepped out. I had never seen him before and, in the deepening shadows of an early fall evening, not well now; but there he was, the man who had taken away my wife and was now stopping by for a little "visitation" of his own. He glanced at my station wagon knowing full well who was in it, then walked to the house. Instead of using the mildly curving bluestone path, he cut straight across the lawn like someone exercising a right. At the front door, maybe he knocked, maybe he didn't. He went in with the ease of someone certain of his welcome. Gail appeared in the open doorway in jonquil yellow. Bleier wrapped his arm around her waist, drawing her in, and— as I watched—he fancifully kicked the door shut...in my face.

That insult has stayed with me all these years. In college I majored in English. Poe was my favorite author, and in one of his stories, "The Cask of Amontillado," the narrator admits that the injuries of Fortunato he could bear, but when it came to insult he vowed to take revenge...and commenced to bury Fortunato in a brick sarcophagus in his wine cellar, alive.

I leave the sandy cove and walk along the beach.

****

Wednesday's group is more of the same. Bleier's technique isn't without success, especially, it would seem, with the women in the circle. At three-thirty, saying he has an important engagement, he lets us out early. Instead of going back to the beach, I leave the path and step onto the cliff, move from one boulder to another toward the ocean. When I come to a reasonably flat rock halfway to the edge, I sit down. A dozen boats with spinnakers of many colors dot the ocean a mile offshore. I seem to think they're in a race—a rainbow regatta—all running with the wind. I try meditating on the roar of the ocean smashing against the rocks, but the pressure in my head, a nameless urgency, won't allow it.

150

THE CLIFF WALK

Seagulls are circling about. A lone bird lands on a boulder beneath the Esalen terrace and some twenty people are coming toward me on the cliff in a scattered, unwieldy group. They're in twos, and one person in each pair has his or her arms outstretched, as if groping for a door in a dark room. The other person stands close by and keeps talking, as if giving instructions, encouragement. Then I realize that the gropers have blindfolds on. Unable to see, they reach out with either the left or right foot and after significant deliberation set it down. In this bizarre manner they all advance—if slowly—over the boulder-strewn cliff.

After some fifteen minutes, blindfolds come down, partners embrace, laugh. Then each pair reverses roles. The gropers become the leaders. And so it goes. When the exercise ends, several people who participated break away, and as a man and woman pass by where I'm sitting, I raise my hand.

"Excuse me."

They stop. "Yes," says the man. He has cut-off jeans on and wears a ponytail.

"I was wondering—what was that all about?"

"It's called the Cliff Walk."

"What's the purpose of it?"

The woman, who has a mop of honey-blond hair, says, "It builds trust."

"How so?"

Ponytail says, "You're blindfolded, some guy is telling you where to walk—what would you call it?"

"I'd hope the guy leading me didn't hate my guts."

The blond laughs. Ponytail gives me a derisive look and they continue on.

****

Halfway through the afternoon session on Thursday, Bleier talks about the Brontsky exercise we'll be doing first thing tomorrow. "So choose someone," he says. "You'll be doing it in pairs."

Group members begin making eye contact, signaling to one another; two people look at me but I shake my head. Then Bleier is talking. "Before we report to the head gardener," he says, "is there anyone at this point who wants to work? We have a little time."

I raise my hand. Bleier says, "Don, good. Come on up."

I go to the center and sit down. Bleier asks me how I'm feeling. I say I'm afraid.

"Of?"

"People. Everyone's out to get me."

"Don, say this. 'I have no trust in my fellow man.'"

"It's so true."

"No, repeat the line," Bleier says.

"I have no trust in my fellow man."

"Now say this, 'I—I want to reach out but I don't dare.'"

"How can you reach out if you're afraid?"

"The line, repeat the line, Don."

"I want to reach out but I can't. I—I'll be rejected. I'm nothing, I'm seaweed."

In the circle a woman in violet pedal-pushers is pressing a handkerchief to her eyes. "Say this," Bleier says. "'The person I really don't trust is myself.'"

"It's the truth."

"The *line*, Don. 'The person I don't really trust—'"

"The Cliff Walk, it petrifies me!"

"We'll be partners," Bleier says. "All right? Now say this—"

"You'll do the Cliff Walk with me?"

"Of course I will, Don."

I reach out and give him a big embrace. "Thank you, Albert."

He doesn't immediately break away; he lets me linger warmly against his chest. Then he says to everyone, "OK, to the garden."

****

Every so often, as I kneel in the soil garden picking kale and stuffing it into a bag, someone in my group comes by and says a few comforting words. I look up and reply, "Thank you, I'm feeling better." In all, we work for two hours. Then, leaving my kale in a large wicker basket, I go up a small hill and open the door to 17. I take a long shower, lie down for thirty minutes, put on fresh clothes and walk to the main building. I haven't seen Penny since morning. I go through the dining hall and step out to the great terrace. Serious socializing is going on; everyone, by now, pretty much knows each other. I don't see Penny and duck into the Elbow Room, just off the terrace. It's a perfect name for the place; it holds twelve people tops. I plan to have a beer but I don't order one. Standing at the little bar with a glass of red wine, talking to a woman with a glass of white wine, is Bleier. The woman, listening attentively, is Penny.

I go back out, find a chair and take in the view. She's interviewing him for her Esalen piece, of course she's attentive; it's her job. People start moving toward the dining-room door. I sit at a table of strangers, all of whom chat brightly among themselves while partaking of their kale, wild rice, sautéed chicken breasts, poached sea bass, tofu and black beans. I finish quickly, deposit my tray at the kitchen window, and return to Room 17. About an hour later Penny walks in.

"I was looking for you at dinner," she says,

"I was there."

"I was in the bar for a while," she said. "Guess who bought me a glass of wine?"

"Albert Bleier. I saw you together."

Penny kicks off her shoes and sits in the easy chair. "He gave me some wonderful stuff on the Institute, the in-fighting that goes on—the different factions. Those who revere Fritz Perls, who lived here in the Sixties, and those who scorn Gestalt Therapy."

"What else did Bleier say?"

"He asked me to go for a drive with him to Carmel-by-the-Sea."

"Were you tempted?"

"I know what Gail saw in him."

"Then you were tempted."

"I'm a married woman," Penny says. "Something your last wife tended to forget."

"Say I hadn't come with you to Esalen—"

"Don, stop it, please!"

"Would you have gone with Bleier to Carmel-by-the-Sea?"

Penny shakes her head sadly. "You're still married to Gail. Nothing has changed in all this time, and it's killing us, Don— you understand that. It's killing us!"

She goes to her desk to review a day's work. I go outside and sit on the bench that overlooks the garden and, somewhere off to the west, a splinter of ocean.

****

At 9:05 a.m. Bleier walks in carrying a gym bag and sits down in the circle. After a little chatter, he begins talking about our upcoming exercise. In his bag, he says, are a bunch of blindfolds. "Putting one on isn't a requirement, though wearing a blindfold enhances the benefits of the exercise, Brontsky and most therapists, including myself, strongly believe. If you're nervous or worried, if you have an anxiety attack, by all means open your eyes and look around, and we'll talk about it when we meet back here after the exercise."

Everyone in the circle is silent. "All right, then," Bleier says, "grab your partner." To me, "Don, let's go."

We follow Bleier across the Oriental bridge, then onto the cliff. It's a cool, overcast day, possibility of rain. Not a soul is out. At a point halfway to the edge, he stops. An onshore breeze is blowing, and whitecaps, countless lambs, frolic on the Pacific.

Bleier hands out blindfolds. "Remember, the name is 'trust,'" he says. "Let it rise up and fill your hearts!"

He gives final instructions. To begin, the person leading should spin the blindfolded person around two times—not to make him or her dizzy, just to add a dimension to the concept of trust. How necessary it is. After ten or fifteen minutes of the exercise, shift roles.

"So, let us begin," Bleier says.

The leaders spin the blindfolded, and the Cliff Walk starts. "Left foot, Judy. More to the left—careful. Good!"

Another member: "OK, Joe. Reach with your right foot—higher. Yes!"

Another: "Barney, your first step requires a big stretch. There's a slight drop, maybe ten inches."

"Which foot?"Barney asked

"Oh, sorry. Right foot."

Bleier watches until all participants are on their way. Satisfied, he says, "Don, let me do the leading to start. Are you up for a blindfold?"

"Not really."

"May I suggest you try?"

"OK, but I'm promising nothing."

Bleier ties it around my head; turning me twice. It has a distinct disorienting effect. "OK, do exactly as I say. Slightly up with your left foot, Don. Steady now." I reach out, set my foot down. "Excellent!" Bleier says.

We're standing on our new perch. I can smell the minty freshness of Bleier's breath. "Now your right foot—down slightly, you have to stretch."

I make it safely. "How am I doing?"

"Superbly," says Bleier.

Left foot, right foot; up, down; big step, little step—it continues. I have no idea of direction. I seem to feel a slightly stronger breeze in my face. "OK, Don," Bleier says, "right foot—this is a big one—I want you to stretch—you can do it."

I hesitate a second. Did Penny tell Bleier my name? Did it accidentally slip out, and Gail's name as well?

"Come on, Don," Bleier says.

I reach out; my foot touches a boulder.

"Great," Bleier says. "I'm proud of you. OK, remove your blindfold."

I pull it down. We're pretty much in the middle of the cliff, about where we started, just farther along. The other teams are a good way ahead. Otherwise, the cliff is empty.

"Trust liberates us in many, many ways," Bleier says. "OK, you lead."

I undo the knot, tie the blindfold snugly around Bleier's head, spin him twice and set a course angling toward the ocean. He follows my instructions perfectly; he's nimble as a mountain goat. "You're doing well, Albert."

"You're marvelously succinct in your commands."

"I wouldn't want you to take a spill."

He laughs. "Lead on."

We take seven, eight more steps, each bringing us closer to the edge. The breeze off the ocean picks up; it's not my imagination. You can almost feel a salty spray on your face. For the first time, Bleier seems tentative, hesitant.

"OK," I say, "left foot, slightly down."

He makes it; we're shoulder to shoulder on a huge rock. A sourness has vitiated his mint-cool breath. "Now just one more and we'll call it a day." We're so near the edge I see waves dashing the rocks below. "Right foot—a really big stretch—"

He doesn't move.

"Albert, come on now, right foot— *reach*—"

He's breathing heavily. How would it look if he tore off the blindfold only to find himself on the cliff, not far from the spot where he started? Not good for our esteemed leader. As I see it, he'll take the step. Anything to protect the ego, his reputation. I say, "Go ahead, Albert. Don't let the group down." My next words are suddenly there. "Do it for Gail, my late wife Gail Williams. She trusted you and you pushed her over the edge. So one last step—*Reach.*"

Bleier rips away the blindfold and looks about, mouth open, eyes wide. Then he glares at me murderously, as well he might, and I set my feet against a boulder. Our little walk on the cliff at Esalen might not be over. "Say this, Albert, repeat after me—"

He lurches away, jumping stiffly from boulder to boulder, almost stumbling. On the shell path Bleier walks hurriedly toward the institute. I move away from the edge. Halfway across the great cliff, I look back at the ocean, then continue on.

He never shows up in our room. People look at me and I have no explanation to give. He split suddenly and left me standing there. Barney from Tucson suggests we all say something by way of our experience at Esalen. Everyone says a few words, mostly in praise of Bleier.

****

The yellow and black minibus arrives at 2:30. About twenty people get on and soon we're on the highway, rolling north. Now and then Penny catches a last view of the coast but mostly she's looking over her piece for *Psychology Today*. With all that she did to wrap it up—last minute shots, quotes, interviews—it's the first time we've been together since breakfast.

"How was the Cliff Walk?" she asks.

"Nothing great. I think it's overrated."

"It's supposed to build trust."

"It's what they say."

Penny takes my hand, holds it for a while, then goes back to her story.

WILDLIFE

On a warm afternoon in early May, Associate Professor Terry Hutchins, home after a day of teaching at New Falls State College, kissed his wife Genevieve affectionately, picked up their three-and-a-half year-old daughter and gave her a big hug, then made himself a vodka and tonic. Drink in hand, he followed the girl out to the rear deck where they would catch the latest episode of "Wildlife," a reality show whose cast lived in, on, or in the vicinity of the six-acre pond behind Terry's house.

He and Colleen sat on a yellow glider that overlooked the pond. It was impossible to say who might star in the day's episode, and his daughter immediately began scanning water and shoreline, eager to see a character she knew. Terry had a taste of his drink and set the glass on a wicker-framed end table. He looked at his daughter, an expression of pride, of adoration on his face. He and Genevieve had both married late, and in time it became clear that they were unlikely to have children. With statistics saying that in vitro fertilization wasn't reliable, they tried it nonetheless and, glory be to God, it worked. They felt blessed when Genevieve gave birth to a beautiful girl.

Terry had another taste of his drink, still on a high from the acceptance of his book on Herman Melville. The editor at NYU had called it an "original, psychologically compelling interpretation of Captain Ahab's maniacal hunt for Moby Dick." Terry was coming up for promotion in the fall, and the publication couldn't be happening at a more opportune time.

He looked out at the pond, more to view and appreciate it than to size up a likely actor. He left all that to Colleen. Most days the water was dull, murky; occasionally, when the afternoon sun hit it just right, it had a lively sparkle. Like now. Scattered about in unruly patches grew loosestrife, locally called "rebel weed," an aggressive plant, seeds of which, Terry had heard, Union soldiers carried in their uniforms on their trek north. Later in the summer a light green algae would appear on the pond. The water was five to six feet deep in places, only two feet near his house, and was fed by a narrow stream, so innocuous a waterway that the town of New Falls called it "Tributary 13." For looks, the pond didn't come near the level of "picture-postcard," but Terry loved it and was happy that Colleen, growing up so close to it, was learning about nature. On several occasions, they had paddled about in his canoe, observing birds, plants, a great variety of creatures. He had told her that Henry David Thoreau, a famous writer and naturalist, drank water straight from Walden Pond. He didn't think Thoreau would recommend drinking the water here.

Suddenly Colleen sang out, "Billy!"

Terry looked across to the far shore. Billy the Muskrat was swimming strongly, his long hairless tail moving back and forth;

in Terry's mind it reminded him of a gondolier's oar. "Today's his day for visiting Aunt Betty," he said.

"Daddy, no. He visited her yesterday."

"But it's Wednesday, it's the day she makes her cherry pies. He knows a good thing."

"Today he's seeing Uncle Lew," Colleen said.

"I'm still thinking Aunt Betty."

"Daddy, Aunt Betty needs rest, doctor's orders. *No visitors.*"

Terry leaned forward as if to get a better look at the muskrat. "Are you sure that's Billy? Maybe it's the doctor."

"Daddy, I know Billy! No one swims like Billy."

"Why is he seeing Uncle Lew? Didn't they have a fight?" Terry said.

"They made up. Billy wants to borrow money from him."

"Colleen, you don't borrow money from someone you've just had a fight with!"

"Billy does."

"Why does he want the money?"

"To buy medicine for Aunt Betty. Look where he's going in." Billy ducked into the base of a large loosestrife. "That's Uncle Lew's house," Colleen said.

"I thought it was Aunt Betty's."

"Daddy, her house is two doors down."

"Oh, so it is."

"You're not paying attention, Daddy."

At any time another character would wander on stage and Terry and Colleen would go at it again, concocting a new, non-sensical scene. Genevieve had commented, more than once, that he was overdoing the fantasy in Colleen's early years. Would she ever take anything seriously? Terry wasn't worried. "Wildlife" was fun, creative. Soon enough, in any event, the novelty of it would wear off.

A couple of red-winged blackbirds flew in and around the loosestrife, and a gray squirrel was scurrying about in the top branches of the big honey locust near the pond. Minor characters. On a slow day, they sometimes got on stage. As the director, editor and producer, Colleen decided.

"Daddy, Mrs. Mallard and her babies are here!"

Terry clapped with delight. The mother duck and her seven ducklings were paddling along in a perfect line, and the young ones had to work hard to keep up. "Just a few days ago they were so tiny," he said.

"They looked like little yellow cupcakes."

He was impressed by the child's figure of speech. "Where have they been?" he wondered out loud.

"Their mommy took them to Disney World," Colleen said. "They met Donald."

"Wow, how exciting! Where did they stay?"

"In the Donald Duck Motel."

Terry laughed.

"Lucy seems tired," Colleen said.

"Who's Lucy?"

"Daddy, the little one at the end of the line."

The duckling had slipped a little behind her siblings. "She's just tired from the trip," he said.

"Come on, Lucy, catch up," Colleen said.

What occurred then drew a cry of outrage from Terry. He half-stood from the glider as if to act, to intercede. A snapping turtle, its neck thick as a gnarled branch, its head the shape of an ill-forged anvil, suddenly rose up, grabbed Lucy's leg in its jaws, then, rolling, sank like a boulder dragging the duckling down. The others scattered. Mother mallard, squawking wildly, fluttered about trying to get her brood back in line.

For a long moment Colleen was silent, stunned, trying to comprehend, to make sense of what had just happened. Then she began screaming, bawling, hands over her eyes as if to blank out what she'd just seen. Terry held her, talking to her quietly, trying to soothe his daughter (and himself). "Colleen," he said, "it—it's all part of nature—"

"Where is she? Where did Lucy go?"

"She—"

"That—that awful monster! Daddy, do something!"

Genevieve came out of the house, alarmed. Badly shaken, he told her what had happened. She picked the horrified child up and went inside. Terry stayed on the deck looking out at the unruffled water....

Two years before Colleen was born, and six months after Terry and Genevieve had moved to New Falls, a local carpenter named Brutus, who was putting a new roof on the house, had told him about a huge snapping turtle that lived in the pond. As a kid he'd fished here for bullheads. Snapper had to be 150 years old. No sooner had Brutus said it than he pointed to a spot roughly in the middle of the pond. The odd swelling of the water there? That's his shell, just below the surface. And eighteen inches in front of the swell, that black thing sticking up like a big chunk of coal? See, it just went under. That's Attila's head.

Attila?

The snapper's name, Brutus said. Who knows who came up with it?

****

163

Not every time Terry sat on his deck after that, but often enough, he would find himself looking to spot Attila. It wasn't that difficult to do. What did a monster snapping turtle have to hide from? Surely not a scholar of 19th century American literature! Terry had come to see Attila as a dark, menacing presence, one that wasn't going to go away anytime soon. In an odd, irrational way, Terry felt threatened. Who was boss around this place? The man who owned the property or some ugly, fearsome reptile?

Colleen was born, and the threat of Attila grew in Terry's mind. Colleen started walking, toddling about with her stuffed animals, and one night he had a nightmare that made him wonder if he and his family would have to move. In the dream, he was going up the deck steps after a day at the college when he saw his daughter out of her playpen, why Terry didn't know, and trundling toward her was Attila. Frozen in fear, Terry struggled to break free so he could run to Colleen and lift her up—the struggle so intense that he woke up in a terrible sweat, screaming. Once Genevieve had calmed him down, she suggested that he see a therapist; clearly Attila was getting the better of his psyche. All told he had five visits with a fine, older woman named Louise who finally made him see that Attila would never, in any conceivable or realistic way, impinge on Colleen's life. He should spare himself further anxiety and go back to his literary musings on Ahab's search for the great white whale. "Do what's within your reach, Terry. Finish your book."

And now Attila's savage attack. Who knew what trauma Colleen had suffered, or how long it would last? He owed it to his daughter and to himself to take action, to end Attila's reign of terror. Terry saw it as a calling, an imperative, to climb down from his Ivory Tower and assume the helm of his own Pequod.

****

On Saturday afternoon, two days later, Genevieve took their still upset daughter to an arts and crafts show on the county fairgrounds, and Terry, alone, launched his mission. From the tool room/workshop attached to the garage, he pulled his green, beloved canoe and carried it to the edge of the pond, then went back for the paddle, his binoculars, and the Remington .22 pump-action rifle he'd had since his boyhood days in Indiana. He loaded the spring-operated magazine with twelve rounds of long-rifle cartridges and, bringing the gun to his shoulders, looked down the open sights at the leaf of a locust tree. As a kid he'd killed many a gray squirrel with a head shot at fifty yards and on one occasion had dropped a grouse in flight—pure luck, a one-in-a-thousand chance, but he'd done it. Terry pushed off in the canoe, binocular strap around his neck, rifle lying at his feet.

He paddled to the middle, then slightly to the left, an area where Attila often lazed sizing up his domain. Terry set the paddle aside. The water was calm, almost no breeze, and his canoe stayed pretty much in the same spot. His favorite way of hunting gray squirrels as a boy was sitting on a fallen tree in the woods and listening for a "tick-tick" in the leaves. Here he was "still hunting" again, this time for different prey. His heart, years ago, was in a quieter place. Hunting squirrels was a sport—the satisfaction of a good shot, the pride of bringing home game. Now he had one driving thought: to put a .22 bullet into Attila's head.

Then, only forty yards away, he saw a mild swelling of the water...and it was coming slowly closer. When Attila's head popped up, Terry reached for the rifle, chambering in a round.

His movements, small as they were, caused the canoe to roll gently—he wasn't sitting on the trunk of a fallen tree—making it difficult to hold aim long enough to make a killing shot. Plus, his arms were shaking. Terry pulled the trigger just as Attila's head disappeared. The bullet zipped by, making a splash. He kept pumping in new rounds, firing nonstop at a spot in front of the heaving water, hoping to injure Attila or at least drive him away. Suddenly the canoe bucked. Water came rushing through the cracked side and bottom, and, tipping, it started to sink. Terry went overboard, the .22 flying from his hand.

Water was up to his chest but the bottom was muddy. Having to half-swim, half-slog to move—more urgently, to get away from Attila, fearful the snapper would take off his hand at the wrist, his foot at the ankle—Terry pushed on, the exertion so great he thought he might have a heart attack. He was floundering, then fell forward, remembering as a kid how Ruff, his arthritic old retriever, had disappeared, and after looking for two days Terry had found him face down in a swampy area behind a neighbor's garage. He righted himself. Coughing up awful-tasting water, he struggled on. The pond became shallower, shore only thirty feet away, and then the bottom seemed to drop out and he pitched forward again and he thought he might drown. He struggled frantically—thrashing, kicking, advancing on sheer will. The bottom of the pond met his feet, and in a last effort Terry reached the mucky shore behind his house. He crawled out like a pre-historic creature and lay there, half-dead.

What finally motivated him to get up was the unhappy thought that his wife and daughter might come home and see him sprawled out on the shore. He did not want to explain, wasn't sure he'd be able to. Terry staggered to the house, stripped off his clothes and dropped them in the garbage can in the garage. Inside, he took a long shower, shampooed vigorously, gargled with a mint-flavored mouth wash, lay down for fifteen minutes, then put on fresh clothes and went out to the deck.

His eyes found the area of the pond where a small section of his canoe, sticking above the surface like a piece of rebel weed torn asunder, marked the spot. He kept looking at the wreckage, then sat back in his chair, wondering if he and Colleen would continue watching "Wildlife." Terry didn't know, but one day, maybe when she was older, he could see himself telling her about an episode she'd missed.

ZERK THE JERK

Every morning a bus would pick up area people going to their defense jobs in Kingsley. It also picked up kids going to the central high school. Four of us—Mr. Hoyt and Mrs. Laidlaw, who made proximity fuses at the Mead plant on Winslow Avenue, and me and Freddie Gould—were waiting for it now. School was just starting; it was the first time since last June that we'd all stood together. Mrs. Laidlaw asked us what we'd done over the summer. I said caddy and Freddy, yawning for the third time, said he'd built a raft. Which was news to me.

Pretty soon we heard the bus working the upgrade past the Vandermark barn on Rt. 257, and a minute later it appeared around the bend, white with black trim and a big 27 on the front, slowed and came to a stop at Rawson Road. The door opened and all of us got on.

The driver was Dennis McCaul. He'd had the Woodridge to Kingsley run for as long as anyone could remember. When he drove, he turned his head to one side because his eyes were crossed, and he always greeted you the same way. "Mornin', neighbor!" Mr. Hoyt and Mrs. Laidlaw dropped into separate seats, Freddie sat with Alex Green near the front, and I went half-way back and sat with my best friend, Jack Kellerhouse.

We had a lot of catching up to do. I'd been away for two weeks with my mother and sister, visiting my father's parents in Green Harbor, Mass. I told Jack about the beach and how you never knew if maybe a U-boat was just off the coast, lurking around. Sometimes I'd wake up at night with the moon shining and look out, hoping I'd see one. I figured the Navy would give me a medal if I reported it.

The bus stopped and a brother and sister, Sylvia and Leroy Quick, got on. They lived in a dark, unpainted house whose roof was covered with pine needles. Jack said, "While you were away, a new boy came to Woodridge."

"Yeah? What's he like?"

"He's a foreigner. His father's on the run."

"On the run?"

"The F.B.I. wants him."

"You kidding me, Jack?"

"Nope. He's a member of the Fifth Column—and his kid's coming to Kingsley High."

"Is he—" I lowered my voice, "—on the bus?"

"Across the aisle, just behind Billy."

I didn't look right away. Then I did. Billy Workman was sitting with his uncle Silas. Behind them was a boy with black hair, a smooth, kind of dark complexion and a straight nose that started high up, almost at his forehead. He was staring through the window with a serious expression on his face.

I came back to Jack. "Who's saying his father belongs to the Fifth Column?"

"Johnny Wilson, at the garage. I was right there. And Billy's father says the same thing."

"What do they base it on?"

"Believe me, they know," said Jack. "Billy's father went out to fix the plumbing—they're renting the Manderville place on Nebraska Quarry Road—and he said he heard this static and squeaking coming from one of the upstairs rooms; and the next thing he knows, Mr. Zerk—that's their name, we call the kid Zerk the Jerk—comes out and starts speaking excitedly in German, and the kid *answers* in German. Then they go in the room together and there's more static, and Billy's dad figured they were getting through to Berlin."

Jack gave his head a small, hard shake. He had a scar on his face from a fishing accident two summers ago when his cousin caught him on the cheek casting a Red-Eyed Wobbler. He'd lost a brother on Okinawa, and every time he walked by the Roll of Honor on the village green he'd stop and touch the gold star by Larry's name. There were other names on it with gold stars also—Richie Cosgrove's, Ted DeCicco's, Al Longendyke's. My father was in the Navy, serving with the J.A.G. in Washington, and there wasn't one of us kids who didn't wish we could join up. But fifteen didn't make it. Older people kept telling us we could do our part, though, by fighting the war at home.

"Anyway," Jack said, "my dad told us to keep an eye on him."

"I guess!"

Dennis maneuvered No. 27 up a narrow, one-way street which brought us to a cinder-covered parking lot behind Kingsley High School. The building was very large, all of dark stone. As we walked toward the boys' entrance, I took another look at Zerk the Jerk. He was about my height, which wasn't that tall, and he had on a long-sleeved white shirt, blue trousers with a nice crease, and polished black shoes.

Our homeroom teacher that year was Wallace A. Russell. He taught science, and he liked to remind you what his initials spelled, in case anyone had the idea of trying to get away with something. As I sat down I noticed Zerk the Jerk at the desk straight across from me and two rows over. The buzzer sounded.

As if daring anyone to make a sound, Mr. Russell waited a few seconds before announcing he would take attendance. He read off about thirty-five names, going through the W's and Y's, and finally said: "Carl Zerk."

Like everyone else, he answered, "Here." The "r" had a heavy kind of roll to it, definitely "foreign." Mr. Russell told us to keep quiet until the next buzzer, at which time we should go to our first classes.

Zerk the Jerk had first-period social studies and sixth-period algebra with me, Jack and Billy, but except to say "Here" in homeroom he never spoke, and after three weeks we were beginning to think the only word he knew was "here." Then Jack came up with the notion, or belief, that he was an apprentice spy under his father. Part of the training he was undergoing, Jack said, was the practice of silence. Zerk the Jerk was a skilled listener, he stored up all the stuff in his head, then spilled it to his dad. I didn't argue the point, only I couldn't imagine what "stuff" Zerk the Jerk could be getting from an ordinary old high school, and Jack said I'd be surprised. The enemy, he said, was very interested in the morale of America's youth, but that was only part of it. What Zerk the Jerk was really after was information about defense jobs—what a kid's parents made, where they worked, where the materiel was heading. And even more important than that, Zerk the Jerk would just love to learn about brothers and fathers in the armed forces—where they were stationed, what their duties were, when they were "moving out." We were all quiet for awhile, wondering what we'd said so far that Zerk the Jerk could've overheard on the bus, in the boys' room or gym.

Then one Monday in mid-October something happened which moved us past talk—to action. Our social studies teacher, Mrs. Kinkaid, asked if anyone in the class could explain the process by which "a bill becomes a law." Usually we went over the homework in class—that is, she explained what we supposedly had read the night before. As a result, no one studied too hard. When no hands went up, Mrs. Kinkaid called on Charlie McLean.

Charlie ran cross-country and was planning on joining the marines on his seventeenth birthday. He stumbled along for fifteen seconds before Mrs. Kinkaid told him to stop. She entered a grade in her book; by the motion of her hand you could tell it was an "F." She looked up. Suddenly we were all very interested in our fingernails.

"Carl."

I expected him to get off the hook by saying he had a language problem—or whatever. But no. Zerk the Jerk started speaking. His accent wasn't so bad as to lose you. What lost you were his choice of words—"constituency," "bicameral," "autonomous." Jack was sitting with his arms folded staring at his inkwell, and Billy's head was lowered and he was giving it tiny shakes. After mentioning the veto powers of the President and the procedure for over-riding a veto, Zerk the Jerk said, "That is how a law is passed in America."

Mrs. Kinkaid was beaming. She called the answer "extraordinarily well expressed, letter perfect." Her hand went to her book and made a distinct "A" with a "+" after it, and later that same day when Zerk the Jerk received the only 100 in the first big algebra test, Jack, me and Billy exchanged glances. Fifteen wouldn't get you to the front, but the front could come to you. This was war!

The next day we called a meeting in the boys' room, with about ten or twelve other guys showing up, for the purpose of forming a club. Its goals were plain and simple. 1. Investigate Zerk the Jerk. 2. Harass Zerk the Jerk. 3. Destroy Zerk the Jerk. I said that properly speaking we were more of a "commission"— I'd heard my father use the term—than a club. It was well taken, and after a brief discussion we decided to call ourselves "The Anti-Zerk Commission."

Jack Kellerhouse was unanimously elected President. Billy Workman was named Vice-president in Charge of Harassment, and I was appointed "Chief Investigator" with the added title of Secret Agent 27 (after our bus). I should begin sitting with Zerk the Jerk two or three times a week, it was decided.

****

"Mornin', neighbor!"

"Morning, Dennis."

There was a chill in the air, and the bus felt warm and comfortable. Jack and Billy were in the back, but instead of continuing down the aisle, I stopped by the empty seat next to Zerk the Jerk. When I sat down he glanced at me, then went back to looking outside.

Jack had told me to go slow, so I didn't talk. Maybe I wouldn't learn anything for a couple of weeks. To move too fast could make a person suspicious. The idea was to win Zerk the Jerk over so when he did open up I'd get some really good stuff. Dennis stopped in West Harleyville and picked up a high school junior named Bob Deets, plus a man and his wife who worked in the factory making radar screens. Then he branched off Rt. 257 onto 82A, which curved and dipped for three or four miles, and by the time we reached the brick viaduct on the city limits the bus was full. The viaduct was steep and very narrow, and coming over it the other way was a big Parson's milk truck. Dennis had to down-shift into low-low, and we just did squeak by.

"That was close!" Zerk the Jerk said, maybe to himself; but I saw the chance to get something going.

"Wait till it snows," I said. "It gets a lot closer than that. One time last winter a fourteen-wheeler hauling scrap metal couldn't make it by. Neither of us could move."

"What happened then?" he asked, really curious.

"Everybody had to get out. We crossed the viaduct on foot and they came for us in a special bus."

Zerk the Jerk was quiet for a few seconds, and I figured that was the end of it, for now. But then he said, "You're Eddie Bishop."

"Right."

"My name is Carl Zerk."

"I know."

We were now over the viaduct and moving along brown, empty streets; uptown Kingsley was a depressing place. "Where do you live?" I asked. Of course I knew.

"On Nebraska Quarry Road. Near the end."

"Then you live near the quarry," I said.

"Do you know it?"

"Sure. It's been a couple of years now, but we used to play there."

"Why do they call it Nebraska Quarry, do you know?"

"The original operators came from Nebraska—that's one story; others say it's the size of it."

Zerk the Jerk seemed friendly, and I saw no trouble in winning his confidence. He asked me what I knew about the old, steam-driven crane.

"The quarrymen left it when they went out of business, about 1900," I said. "My father said it was cement—suddenly no one wanted bluestone anymore."

"So they just deserted the crane?"

"What were they going to do with it?"

"I was up there last Sunday looking at it," Zerk the Jerk said. "It's really a beautiful thing!"

I viewed it as a heap of rusty metal, but I saw no point in disagreeing with him. At noontime the Anti-Zerk Commission met in the boys' room, and I reported that I was off to a good start. Pretty soon I should have some hot information. Jack said to keep it up, then asked Billy how he was coming along on his harassment campaign. Billy said that he and his right-hand man, Charlie McLean, had discovered that Zerk the Jerk's homeroom desk was neat as a pin, and they figured it would be a good place to begin. Jack said those were excellent ideas. Psychological warfare, like that, often had more effect on the enemy than beating on him physically. It was nothing to wish for, but sometimes I wished I had the scar on my cheek that Jack had, from the Red-Eyed Wobbler. It gave him a look, and whenever he talked, we listened.

I let two days go by before sitting with Zerk the Jerk again, this time on the ride home. His eyes brightened when I shoved my books in the rack above the seats "Hi, Eddie. How's it going?" he said.

"Pretty good, Carl."

I sat down. Jack got on the bus and walked by, and in another minute Dennis pulled out of the school parking lot. I told Zerk the Jerk I wasn't getting algebra, specifically how to work a problem with two unknowns. He said he'd show me. Using paper and pencil, he did three problems for me, step by step, until I caught on. "Okay, you do one," he said, writing down a problem and passing me his notebook. I solved it in twenty seconds.

"See how easy it is?"

"Now that I understand. Thanks."

Dennis turned left on Rondout Avenue, heading west toward Woodridge. Zerk the Jerk began a new conversation by telling me he'd been studying steam.

"Studying steam?" I didn't know what he was talking about.

"I've been reading up on it," he said. "My father has a couple of books and I got two more out of the village library." He paused. "I figure if I learn enough about the properties of steam, maybe I can get the old crane running again."

I gave the boy sitting next to me a long, slow look. *"What?"*

"Maybe I can get the old crane going again."

"It's rusted all to hell. It's a piece of junk!"

"It's rusted, yes, but it's not junk, Eddie. My father went over the boiler with a hammer. He said he wouldn't want to put it under a full head of steam, but it's still sound."

Of all the wild, far-fetched ideas! Whether Zerk the Jerk was an "apprentice spy" I still didn't know, but I suddenly had the feeling he was a little crazy. "If you want my opinion—"

"I was wondering if you'd help me."

"Help you?"

"Sure. The whole job might take a couple of years, but just think when we got it going!"

I gave my forehead a rub. "OK, let's say we got it going. Then what?"

"Who knows? Maybe we'd just have fun with it, chugging around the quarry blowing the whistle."

Was this kid for real? I told him I'd let him know—I'd think it over.

At the next meeting of the Anti-Zerk Commission, I brought up the topic of the crane in the Nebraska Quarry, saying that Zerk the Jerk wanted me to help him get it going again. The Kingsley kids like Charlie McLean had no point of reference on this, so they didn't comment, but Billy Workman said my job as a Secret Agent was to investigate Zerk the Jerk, not to get mixed up in some stupid project! There was a war going on. Our job was to destroy the enemy, and playing games with Zerk the Jerk in Nebraska Quarry wasn't how to do it. I thought Jack would agree. He thought awhile, then said that Billy was wrong. Working with Zerk the Jerk on the crane was a golden oppor-tunity, he said. In time, he'd probably have me inside his house. I would meet his mother and father. I'd be able to look around, to really investigate the Zerk family. Billy was nodding; he saw where he was wrong. Jack looked at me and said, "Tell him you'll do it, Eddie."

I did, sitting with him that afternoon on the bus. He was a happy kid. "How about starting tomorrow?" Zerk the Jerk said.

Tomorrow was Saturday. I said, "Sure."

"Why don't you come for lunch," he said.

****

The house was a big rambling place weathered to a dark-brown through the years, with probably a dozen rooms. It sat on a ridge above the village, with fields and woods surrounding it. Zerk the Jerk met me in the driveway as I rode up on my bike and right away told me what we were having, as if to prepare me or something. Green peppers stuffed with rice, ground meat and onions; and baklava. Whatever it all was, it didn't sound German. "Come on in," he said.

His mother was in the kitchen, which was very big—the size of our living room at home. She had dark, shiny hair, very smooth skin, and a nose like her son's. Between them was a strong resemblance. Except for their accents. Hers was totally different—thinner, you might say, less roll to the letters. She welcomed me warmly, then told her son that lunch wasn't ready, why didn't he show Eddie around. It occurred to me I was doing OK.

The first room Zerk the Jerk took me to was the "library." It was on the main floor and had big windows opening to the fields. I'd never seen so many books at the same time except in a *real* library. One shelf had about twenty volumes just on radios, a lot of the titles in German; it was incriminating evidence, to say the least. Then Zerk the Jerk showed me sections of the library devoted to music, physics, engineering, ships, and machinery. And finally "the classics." I wasn't sure what "the classics" meant, but I didn't want to appear dumb by asking. It did, however, seem like a good time to ask Zerk the Jerk what his father did for a living.

"He's a conductor."

"On a train?"

"No, Eddie. Of orchestras!" He moved his arms and hands.

"Oh."

"But he has lots of other interests. Let's go upstairs."

Zerk the Jerk's room had two beds in it and two large windows. It was clean, orderly, what my mother called "picked up." His school books were stacked on a small oak desk. He had his own book shelves. One of them was filled with copies of *National Geographic*. He said he'd been getting the magazine for four years, and he'd read every one from cover to cover. Hanging from the ceiling on strands of thread were model airplanes he'd made—a P-47 Thunderbolt, a Zero, a Messerschmitt. At present he was working on a P-38 Lightning. To my eye, each model seemed a work of perfection, and I wondered how Zerk the Jerk could study his lessons and still find time to read *National Geographic* and construct model planes. We went out to the hallway, which was a long balcony overlooking the main sitting room. He asked me if I was interested in seeing his father's newest project.

"Sure. Is he home?"

"No, he's in Chicago."

Zerk the Jerk opened a door at the end of the balcony; inside, on a long table, were the makings of a radio. You could see all the components, the tubes and wires. On the table, also, were several diagrams or blueprints and three or four open books. Other radios and related equipment were scattered about the room. Why Zerk the Jerk would be showing me all this stuff if his father had ties with the Germans seemed odd.

"My father's developing a new high-fidelity receiver," he said. "When it works it's like a bell. It's so clear and static-free it's eerie. But he still has a ways to go."

"Where did he learn all this?"

"It's been a life-long interest. My dad was the first person to ever assemble a radio in Albania."

"Albania?"

"It's my mother's homeland."

"Oh. Where is it?"

"Yugoslavia is to the north and Greece is to the south, and everywhere you look there's a mountain. And goats. All you ever see in Albania are mountains and goats."

"What happened to the radio?"

"The authorities found out about it and confiscated it."

"How come?"

"They thought it was dangerous. They asked us to leave."

"Did you?"

"We all went back to Austria."

"Why there?"

"That's my father's homeland. I was born there."

"You're not—*German?*"

"No, Austrian. And Albanian."

Zerk the Jerk pointed to a black, boxy radio across the room. "That's my father's short-wave set, Eddie. A couple of nights ago we got Moscow; and we're always picking up Tokyo Rose."

I didn't know what to say. Just then his mother called that lunch was ready. "Maybe some night you can sleep over," Zerk the Jerk said. "We'll be able to listen."

****

The quarry was just over a rise in the road from the Zerks' house. We went there after lunch, with Zerk the Jerk carrying a pack in which he had put a couple of wire brushes, an assortment of chisels and chipping hammers, an oil can with a flexible spout, and three or four books and pamphlets on steam-driven machinery; but best of all (as I thought) he had also put in four extra squares of baklava.

At a point fifty yards beyond the rise we cut off the road onto a wood trail, followed it for a minute, and suddenly we were standing at the edge of the Nebraska Quarry. It was a quarter-mile across, maybe more, and everywhere you looked was rubble. Chunks and pieces of bluestone. It was hard stuff, perhaps the hardest stone known to man; ten-thousand winters, an old-timer once told me who knew such things, wouldn't touch or change it. A rough road wound from the top of the quarry to a spring-fed lake at the bottom, and approximately mid-way between the two points stood the crane.

Looking at it, I immediately recognized what I had known all along—how pointless it was even *trying* to get it going. The crane was a relic from an earlier day, a broken, battered skeleton. Bringing wire brushes to work on it was like arriving at the site of a proposed tunnel with a coal shovel.

"Isn't it a beauty, Eddie?" Zerk the Jerk said. "Just think when we get it fired up!"

"Right."

Rather than follow the spiraling road, we cut straight across the great excavation. The rubble was securely lodged, but you had to watch your step, go easy. From the lake three mallards suddenly took off and flew away. Thick woods surrounded the quarry, except for an area to the south opening toward the village, and all the leaves were in full color. When we reached the crane Zerk the Jerk set his pack on the rocks, opened it and took out a book called *Principles of Steam Locomotion.* He laid it carefully on one of the knobbed steel wheels, read, looked up at the machinery, then read some more. Next he studied a couple of drawings, again looking up and down between crane and book. How the stuff meant anything to him was amazing.

"Okay," he said, "here's the deal."

The first thing he pointed out was the boiler, a cylinder ten times the size of your hot water tank at home; its weight served as a counter-balance, the reason it sat on the *rear* of the crane. The long neck was called the jib. It was raised and lowered—he was pointing—by a cable attached to a drum. The cable wasn't broken but it looked very worn, with a thousand little spurs in it that resembled fishhooks.

Zerk the Jerk grabbed hold of a rusty steel shaft about the thickness of the handle of a baseball bat. "This is called the eccentric rod, Eddie," he said. "It cuts off the flow of steam to the drive shaft, *here*, so the flywheel, *here*, can make a full revolution. Otherwise the flywheel would never get back into position."

"Position? For what?"

"To make the power stroke."

He broke out the tools. "OK, you tackle the eccentric rod. Try and get it to bare metal. I'll do the main shaft."

At first I was bored, thinking I'd much rather be in the woods with my .22, but after a while I got in a kind of rhythm, and what with Zerk the Jerk's stories about growing up in Austria and spending summers in Albania, the time passed quickly. Personally, I didn't see any progress but he told me Rome wasn't built in a day. We'd made a good start. He suggested we take a break down by the lake.

We sat on flat pieces of bluestone by the water's edge and ate our baklava; it was flaky and sweet with nuts in it and was the best thing I ever tasted. Zerk the Jerk said it had twenty layers of crust, each rolled and smoothed out separately. In the lake you saw the reflection of the sky and you could see, without looking up, a hawk swooping overhead. Zerk the Jerk said his father had once trained falcons in Austria and was thinking about doing it again. We finished the baklava and were quiet for awhile. There wouldn't be many days, Indian summer days like this, left. There was no way of knowing a war was going on.

"Eddie." Zerk the Jerk was making a design on a piece of bluestone with a smaller piece. Without looking up, he said, "The kids say things about me, don't they?"

It occurred to me that I hadn't thought of the Anti-Zerk Commission once all day. "Sometimes they do."

"Both my parents are American citizens. They love this country," he said.

He *could* be saying that, I reasoned, to throw me off. There was no way of knowing a war was going on, but one *was* going on. I had to remember that. I was a member of the commission.

"Do you know something, Eddie?"

"What, Carl?" In the deep woods above the quarry a gray squirrel was crying.

"Having a friend is a good thing," he said.

****

On the following Tuesday Zerk the Jerk found his homeroom desk stuffed with trash and garbage when he opened it in the morning. I was sitting at my own desk and knew what to expect, because Billy had told me the day before. For a few seconds Zerk the Jerk stared at the mess, then, quietly and slowly, lowered the top, as if nothing was wrong; but you could see his chest move and his eyes were straight ahead and squinting. I looked away. At noontime the Commission met, and people congratulated Billy and Charlie McLean on their first harassment. Then they wanted to know how I was coming along with my investigation.

"The Zerks aren't German," I said. "They're Austrian—except for the mother. She's an Albanian."

"A *what?*"

"It's between Yugoslavia and Greece."

"Go ahead," said Jack.

"It's important, I think, that Mr. Zerk is Austrian," I said.

"Austrian, German—it's all the Axis," Jack said, getting angry. "They speak the same language! What else?"

"I saw Mr. Zerk's radios. It's a hobby with him, you might say. He's developing a system without any static. Then they have a short-wave set, he built it himself—but all they do is listen."

No one said anything. Everyone just stared at me. Then Jack said, "Right—all they do is listen!"

"I didn't see any transmitters," I said.

"You're sure of that?"

My face was starting to feel hot. "I am, yes!"

"Well next time you're in the Zerks' house, take a better look!"

Other harassments followed. On one occasion Charlie McLean found Zerk the Jerk's locker opened and poured rubber cement in his sneakers. Instead of explaining to Mr. Jeffrey, the gym teacher, he didn't show up and took an absence. Then several days later he left his lunch on a cafeteria table to get a container of milk, and when he returned it was gone. I wasn't there but I learned about it. When the Commission met the next morning, Jack said Zerk the Jerk was starting to crack. He looked at me. How was I doing? Anything new?

I said I was getting a lot of information together. He said good. At this rate, we should have Zerk the Jerk destroyed by Christmas.

****

Whether we would or wouldn't, I didn't know, but Carl and I kept working on the crane. On one occasion Mr. Zerk came with us to the quarry. He had snowy hair, longer than you usually saw on a man, and a round, friendly face. He didn't stay long, maybe fifteen minutes, just to see how we were doing. He had a heavy accent but I couldn't see him as a spy, and on another occasion when it began raining he put my bike in the back of his Packard and drove me home, the three of us in the front seat. The weather turned cold; then one day Zerk the Jerk produced a can of special oil designed to "eat through rust," which his father had bought for us in Detroit. We used the entire can but still, no matter how hard we yanked and tugged, we couldn't get the fly wheel to turn. We stood by the crane, late that afternoon, panting. Zerk the Jerk's head was lowered. He was thinking and I let him think. Something good was bound to come out of it. All the leaves were brown now, those that remained, and soon ice would cover the ake.

"We need a mechanical advantage," he said at last.

It sounded reasonable. "OK."

We went back to his house and he found a long 2x4, and when we returned he inserted an end in the fly wheel. The other end angled out, and he jumped up and pulled down on it; it splintered, and Zerk the Jerk fell on the rubble, hard.

"Are you all right, Carl?

He was holding his knee, kind of grimacing. "I'm OK."

"Maybe we should quit for today."

Zerk the Jerk looked up at the fly wheel. Then he said, "I have it, Eddie. There's a block and tackle hanging in the garage."

"Will that help us?"

"With a four-to-one ratio? You bet it will."

What a monster it was, two pulleys the size of footballs and a ton of rope—and what a job lugging it back to the quarry. We hooked one of the blocks to the fly wheel and the second to the frame; together we picked up the loose end of rope and drew the tackle taut.

"Are you ready?" Zerk the Jerk said.

"I'm ready."

"Okay, Eddie. Pull!"

We pulled, and we tugged, and we heaved.

"Pull, Eddie!"

"Jesus Christ, I'm pulling!" My eyes were closed.

"Pull harder!"

"I'm pulling harder—"

Then something seemed to give, not all at once but slowly, as if the rope was rubber and we were stretching it; we took two steps backward, still holding on—except now the rope was slack.

"Eddie, we did it!" cried Zerk the Jerk.

"We did?"

"Look at the block."

At the start it had been at the top of the fly wheel; now, still hooked on, it was at the bottom. The wheel had made one-half of a revolution. You should have seen us, dancing about on the rubble and shouting. Then Zerk the Jerk was hugging me. I'd never seen a kid so happy.

We sat down to rest, sweating, our hands sore from pulling on the rope. On the knee of his pants was a dark, wet stain. Then he looked at me and said he had an idea.

"What is it?" In the big woods came the report of a high-po-wered rifle.

"The war's not going to last forever," he said. "My father says another year. So listen to this. By then, we should have the crane operating, right? And I was thinking we could reactivate the quarry. People will be wanting stone. For sidewalks, founda-tions, for general construction. We'd have a heck of a business, Eddie! What do you think?"

I didn't know what to think, it all seemed so distant and far away; but it occurred to me that whatever ability Carl Zerk had to dream, I didn't have. And I didn't know anyone else who had it, quite like that. Certainly my pals from Woodridge and the kids in Kingsley High didn't have it. You didn't form Anti-Zerk Commissions on dreams, I saw that clearly now. You formed them out of fear.

"It sounds great," I said.

"We'll call ourselves BISHOP & ZERK, Inc."

I didn't know why he would put the word "ink" after our names, but there had to be a reason; I didn't question it. We shook hands, then sat there for a while, kind of daydreaming, I suppose. Ten minutes later we left the quarry and went back to his house. As we walked into the kitchen, Zerk the Jerk asked me if I could spend the night. We could finish his P-38, he'd show me some of his all-time favorite articles in *National Geographic,* and later on we might get lucky and catch Tokyo Rose.

I missed the next four days with a fever and sore throat. My mother said it was from working on the crane, from sweating and then sitting down in the cold. Carl called me every afternoon when he got home to give me homework assignments but mostly to talk. I wanted to hear what was going on in school but he didn't say much; it was almost like he didn't care. He had other things to think about. Like the crane. After school he went to the quarry and worked on it for an hour. The fly wheel was pretty free now, he said. You could turn it by hand.

"That's great, Carl."

"I have a surprise for you," he said.

"A surprise?"

"Yes."

"What is it?"

"It's a surprise, I said."

"Give me a hint."

"It has to do with the crane. What else?"

****

"Mornin', neighbor!"

"Morning, Dennis."

It was my first day back and I glanced down the aisle. Jack and Billy were sitting in the back, as always. The look they gave me when I stopped by Zerk the Jerk's seat—well, it said they knew. That was all. They knew.

"Hi, Carl," I said.

"Eddie, how you feeling?"

"Better. I'm OK."

That morning as we were going to first-period class, I noticed ten or twelve kids gathered around Zerk the Jerk in the corridor. He was standing by his locker, needing something before going to Social Studies, but he wasn't making any attempt to open it. Then I saw why. Hanging from the dial on the combination lock was a Trojan. I'd seen a new one; this one didn't look new.

The guys were snickering and making comments, and Zerk the Jerk seemed lost as to what to do; he didn't look angry, just bewildered. "What's the matter, Jerk, forget the combo?" Charlie McLean said.

"Leave him alone," I said.

"Nazi sympathizer! Who you talking to?"

"You. Leave him alone."

Charlie ambled over. He was tall and skinny. "You gonna make me?" he said.

I didn't answer. I made a fist and let him have it. He staggered against the lockers, blood squirting from his nose. Then Jack jumped me and I gave him a shot also. Ninety-nine teachers came running up. Next thing I knew I was talking to Mr. Glass, the principal, in his office.

He wanted to know what had happened. I said kids were harassing Carl Zerk and I didn't like it. That wasn't my job, he said. If I ever fought on school property again he'd suspend me for two weeks. I should go to class. Waiting outside, also there to see Mr. Glass, was Jack. He had a dark-blue welt under his eye, and he hissed a single word at me. "Traitor." I came close to getting the two-week suspension, then and there.

All morning there was talk. You saw Jack and Billy on the stairs, in the boys' room, their heads together with other guys on the Commission. By third period Charlie McLean was back from the nurse's office, a wad of gauze stuffed in his nose.

At noontime Carl sat with me in the cafeteria. I didn't feel like talking and he didn't force a conversation. Then, just before we left, he said, "They can't touch us, Eddie."

That was nice to think, but I didn't see how twenty kids couldn't "touch" two—unless Carl had something up his sleeve. The afternoon passed slowly. In algebra class Miss Fuller announced that Carl Zerk had the highest average for the marking period just ended, with a 98. Second was Anne Winke with a 93; and third Louise Benjamin with an even 90. Most improved, she said, was Edward Bishop, who had jumped from a 71 to an 88 average. As was her custom at such times, she handed out gold stars, with instructions to paste them in our notebooks.

I looked across at Carl. He gave me a thumbs-up. When the class ended, everyone began drifting out. I thought he might stop and, actually, expected him to, but he was in a rush. He had Latin last period and probably wanted to review the assignment. Carl dropped a folded piece of paper on my book and kept going.

It was our strategy! I sat for a few seconds, thinking Carl Zerk had to be the smartest, the bravest kid who'd ever lived. Then I unfolded the slip of paper and read his note—and read it again—and then again. I couldn't believe what he'd written.

A girl wanted my desk and I stood up and walked out and went to homeroom for seventh-period study hall. Only you can bet I didn't study. I sat there, lost, bewildered. Carl's note explained everything—the way he would put his arm around me every so often, how he had called me when I was sick, how he had hugged me when we'd finally turned the fly wheel over, the way he'd sat on my bed the night I'd slept at his house until two in the morning. It all fit. And _I_ was the jerk for not seeing it, for not realizing what his friendliness meant.

I read the note again. "Remember, Eddie, they can't touch us. You're my best friend, future partner, and a great Homo sapiens. Carl."

The way "sapiens" sounded, you knew it was a special kind, probably _his_ kind of homo. I crushed the note in a ball and chucked it inside my desk.

Seventh period ended and I didn't look over when Zerk the Jerk came in and sat down. Mr. Russell made a few announcements, the last buzzer sounded, and everyone left. I disappeared into the boys' room, not wanting to walk out with Zerk the Jerk. Three minutes later I went outside, and as I approached the parking lot I saw what I had expected all day to see—a gang of boys tightly gathered around the back of No. 27. Zerk the Jerk was in the center, and I hated to admit it—he had guts. He was holding his own. I heard him say he'd fight everybody there, one a time.

Even as he spoke, he kept looking toward the school. Then all at once everyone saw me. The gang opened up, as if to get both me and Zerk the Jerk in the middle. Thinking his reinforcements had arrived, he came up to me and started to say something—and I gave him a push. Everyone was stunned, and Carl looked at me with an expression of total confusion. He came toward me again, and this time I punched him in the chest, hard, and he fell back against the bus.

"That's for getting me wrong!" I yelled at him.

He stood there, just staring at me, and then, slowly, his face broke. It seemed to go into a thousand pieces. One hand was on his chest, where I'd hit him, and as if from beneath that spot there came a deep, a terrible sound. Tears sprang to his eyes, and the next moment he was running, away from the bus and the school, toward the street.

The guys thought it was wonderful. They congratulated me, pounding me on the back and shoulders, suddenly seeing what I'd been up to all this time: pretending to befriend Zerk the Jerk, even as to fool the Commission, so as to more effectively achieve its goals. It was hard for Charlie McLean, but he came up and said he didn't hold any grudges. I'd done one fantastic job as a secret agent. Then Jack said I wasn't rightly an agent at all, but a *double* agent. He was going to write our Congressman in Washington so I could get a medal. I looked toward the street. Then we all got on the bus, and everyone was wild going home, and twice Dennis had to shout at us to keep it down. Zerk the Jerk didn't come to school for the next couple of days, and about a week later we heard that the family had moved.

There were rumors as to where. Chicago was mentioned, Southern California, even Mexico, but the reasons for the move were always the same; the F.B.I. was closing in on Mr. Zerk. People in Woodridge said it was strong evidence that he really did have ties with the Fifth Column.

I didn't get a medal but, in a manner of speaking, I was a kind of hero for the rest of the year. In May we were all saddened when a gold star appeared beside the name of Wilbur Shultis, the J.P.'s son; but later in August there was rejoicing when America dropped an atom bomb on Japan. Very soon after that, the war ended. We had parades in the streets, and my father made a speech standing in his lieutenant commander's uniform by the Roll of Honor, praising all the men and women of Woodridge who, in answering the call to the colors, had helped bring victory to America. And he praised those of us who had fought the war at home. Jack Kellerhouse looked over at me and grinned.

****

But from time to time, as I entered my third year and then became a senior, I would find myself thinking about Carl. On rainy or snowy afternoons, I might look through a classroom window and find myself reliving that day he had handed me the note, and I would feel the hurt, anger and confusion all over again. On more than one occasion I dreamed the scene by the bus, as he came toward me, as I punched him in the chest and his face shattered. Then I would awaken, and lie there, and wonder where he was; and I seemed to know that something was unanswered, unfinished, between me and Carl Zerk. But what, I didn't know. Perhaps it would be one of those mysteries, those puzzles, that stay with you forever.

I went to college in my first car, a 1936 "straight-8" Buick that had a rumble seat and burned a quart of oil every hundred miles. I made new friends, went to football games, and fell in love with a girl with light-brown hair who wore long colorful scarves. I enjoyed my courses, except for Introduction to Anthropology. The professor rambled on, often losing himself in the middle of a sentence. He was a friendly old guy and occasionally said something interesting, but mostly he put you to sleep. It was the third week of the semester, and I was dozing in the October-lighted room.

"—in his latest stage of development," he was saying, "capable of thinking, knowing. In the most universal sense—*wise man.*"

Professor Werner paused. I didn't know what he was talking about but my heart, oddly, began pounding. "I have always taken the term as a symbol," he went on, "describing what we are all capable of becoming. It applies to everyone but only fits a few. Nevertheless, we should all feel proud to come under so noble a heading as *Homo sapiens.*"

My hands came together over my face; my head dropped. A few moments later I got up and left the room.

Later that day I drove home, stopping only to add another quart of 50-weight oil to my car. My parents were surprised when I pulled in at eleven o'clock. Was something wrong? I said I was feeling a little lonely, but nothing was wrong. I'm not sure they believed me. The next morning, before breakfast, I drove into Woodridge, following the road up into the hills above the village.

I drove slowly past the Zerks' house. It was dark and still, and smaller than I remembered it. Just beyond the house I parked, got out, and walked to the opening of the quarry.

The trees, surrounding it, were jacketed in many colors, and in one of the great hickories at the far end a hundred crows were holding an early morning caucus. The lake was covered with leaves. My eyes shifted, and I was looking at the crane.

I started across the great heaps and piles of broken bluestone. Having decided on what they had to decide, the crows suddenly flew away, and the quarry was quiet. I continued on carefully and in a few minutes was standing beside the crane. It was already too old, broken and rusted for anything to have changed.

I examined the eccentric rod. Would I ever forget that it stopped the flow of steam so the fly wheel could make a complete revolution? I took a deep breath. Then I glanced at the cab.

Something seemed different about it, though I couldn't tell what. I kept looking, trying to decide, and finally realized that, all these years a mere frame, the cab now had a piece of siding attached to it—a 2'x3' section of sheet metal. It was rusted, but beneath the rust a faint red haze shone through, like the first glimmer of a sunrise. Then I saw that the haze was paint and the paint represented words. I moved closer and suddenly the words jumped out: BISHOP & ZERK, Inc.

The letters blurred. In my chest I felt a deep, a terrible ache, and from that spot rose the beginnings of an agonized sound, which somewhere I had heard before.

Anthony Robinson, author of seven novels, taught literature and creative writing at SUNY New Paltz for thirty-four years. Now retired, he lives on Huguenot Street in New Paltz with his wife, Tatiana.

Made in the USA
Charleston, SC
13 November 2013